LOST TREASURES

Merlin's Mistake

ROBERT NEWMAN

D1374248

VOLO

HYPERION
NEW YORK

If you purchased this book without a cover, you should be aware that this book is stolen property. It was reported as "unsold and destroyed" to the publisher, and neither the author nor the publisher has received any payment for this "stripped book."

Text © 1970 by Robert Newman

First published by Atheneum © 1970. Reprinted by permission of
The Estate of Robert Newman

Volo and the Volo colophon are trademarks of
Disney Enterprises, Inc.
All rights reserved. No part of this book may be reproduced or transmitted in any form or by any means, electronic or mechanical, including photocopying, recording, or by any information storage and retrieval system, without written permission from the publisher. For information address Volo Books, 114 Fifth Avenue, New York,
New York 10011-5690.
First Volo Edition, 2001

1 3 5 7 9 10 8 6 4 2

The text for this book is set in 13-point Deepdene.

ISBN 0-7868-1545-0
Library of Congress Catalog Card Number on file.

Visit www.volobooks.com

On Merlin's insistence:

For Gerry

CHAPTER ONE

ALTOGETHER IT HAD been a strange spring. About Candlemas one of the kitchenmaids became convinced that the cook was the devil and fled screaming into the great hall where the Lady Leolie boxed her ears and poured a goblet of cider over her head to quiet her. This had so upset the cook that he had not been able to bake a proper pasty until after Lent. During Whitsuntide the alewife's brindle cow had a calf with two heads, and shortly after that a strange, bearded comet appeared in the midnight sky and burst into a flaming shower directly over the castle. Disturbing as these portents were—and since it would soon be Midsummer Eve there would probably be more of them—the worst part about them was that no one, not even Father Bernard, could tell what they meant. Only Brian thought he knew.

On this particular morning the sun had awakened him. Slanting in through the narrow window of the tower room, it shone full on his face. He stirred, blinked and finally sat up. But even before he remembered what day it was, he was filled with an odd excitement. It was of course a very important day: his birthday. He was now sixteen and a man. Or almost a man. But he had a feeling that there was more to it than that.

Staring at the shaft of sunlight, he seemed to see his mother, the Lady Leolie, standing in the courtyard with Sir Guy beside her. They watched as he mounted his horse and—at long last—rode through the gatehouse and across the drawbridge out into the world. Was that why he felt as he did? Had he been dreaming about it just before he woke? It was very vivid, very real. But then he had had that same dream so often when he was awake that he could not be sure.

The straw of the pallet rustled as he got up and hurried across the stone floor to the window. The villeins' cottages, the fields and the pastures all lay west of the castle, on the other side of the tower. On this side there was just the forest. And since his room was on a level with the tops of the trees, he looked out on a sea of green that steamed as the summer sun burned off the early morning dew. The forest began a bowshot beyond the moat and extended as far as the eye could see. Even from the top of the tower, he could not see its end. It looked more like a sea than ever from there, with the castle and its land an island lapped by the living green.

Leaning out the window, he looked to his left. He could not have said who or what he expected to see. But possibly because most of those who visited Caercorbin—an occasional knight, monk or chapman—came from the North, for some time now he had been convinced that it was from that direction that the harbinger of his freedom—and his great adventure—would come. Nothing stirred on the forest track. But since he could see only a short distance because of the trees, that meant nothing.

He pulled on his hose, tunic and shoes, buckled his belt and went quietly down the stairs. Though his mother was an early riser, she was not yet awake; and Agnes, his old nurse who slept in the solar outside her room, did not see him as he went by. Two serving wenches, still lying near the hearth, looked up sleepily as he hurried through the great hall and out into the courtyard. At that moment he heard the rattle and rumble of the drawbridge as it thudded down, the creak of the heavy outer doors. The doors were only partly ajar when he reached them and slipped through, startling the two men-at-arms who were pulling them open.

"Ho there, Brian," called Simon, Sir Guy's

squire, from the gatehouse. "Where are you going?"

Brian waved to him without answering, then he was over the drawbridge, running across the open ground that surrounded the moat and into the forest.

For a space the underbrush had been cleared away so that there would be no cover for an enemy. The grass was still wet with dew, and it soaked his shoes as he loped under the branches of the huge oaks. A rabbit started up ahead of him and fled to his hole, and off to his right a partridge rose drumming and flew low and straight into a tangle of bracken. He was in a copse of beeches now, trotting along an almost invisible trail. Then there was the knoll, covered with grass and patches of gorse. He climbed up it quickly and, when he reached the top, he paused for the first time since leaving his room.

This was one of his favorite spots in the forest. Lying hidden among the rocks on its top, he could watch the comings and goings of the animals: the deer, the wild boars, the badgers and the foxes. But even better, from here he could see far more of the narrow track that led to Caercorbin than he could from the castle's highest tower. Shielding his eyes, he again looked north. Still nothing. He was about to turn away when he saw a glint of metal far up the road where it began to curve. Then, as he watched, three figures came into sight. The first, mounted on a gray palfrey, seemed rather small, but he was richly dressed in a blue tunic and cape. Two varlets in steel caps and leather jacks rode behind him; it was the gleam of the sun on their helmets that had first caught Brian's eye.

He continued watching as they drew nearer. The two varlets wore the Ferlay blazon, and all three of them rode slowly as if they were weary. Suddenly Brian stiffened. Something moved in the underbrush on the near side of the track. There were other movements on the far side. They would have been invisible from the road, but they could be seen clearly from the top of the knoll, and Brian knew what they meant: Long Hugh and some of his men were waiting there to waylay the travelers.

Scrambling up the nearest rock so he would be visible against the sky, Brian put his fingers to his lips and whistled shrilly. Then, as the lurking figures turned, he waved his arm like a falconer calling off a hawk. For a moment the men below him hesitated. Then the tallest one waved back and they melted into the bushes.

When they heard his whistle, the three riders reined in their horses and looked up also, the two varlets reaching for their swords. Brian waved again, reassuringly this time, then went running down the knoll toward them.

They were still waiting when he reached the narrow road. The gray horse shied when Brian appeared out of the underbrush, and his rider had to check and quiet him. He was a somewhat solemn-looking, dark-haired boy, two or three years younger than Brian.

"Greetings," he said. "You startled us. We did not know that there was anyone about."

"That was partly why I whistled," said Brian. "Because there were others about besides me."

"What do you mean?" asked the boy. Then he glanced into the underbrush, looked at Brian again and said, "I see. May I ask who you are?"

"I am Brian, son of Sir Owaine of Caercorbin."

"Caercorbin? I told you it could not be much farther," he said to the varlets.

"That's what you've been saying since sunset last night," said one of the varlets sullenly.

"And, as you can see, I was right. But since we are so close now, you need not come any farther."

Immediately the varlet who had spoken, a red-bearded man, turned his horse. But the other one hesitated.

"We can't leave you yet, master. Sir Gerard told us to see you safely there."

"It is only about a mile," said Brian. "And I will be with him."

"Very well, then," said the second varlet, and he turned his horse also.

"Wait," said the boy, reaching into the pouch on his belt. "Take this for your trouble." He gave him some coins. "With my thanks."

"Thank you, master," said the varlet, raising a knuckle to his forehead. Then the two spurred their horses and went cantering off back the way they had come.

"A surly pair," said Brian. "At least the one with the red beard was."

"They were uneasy," said the boy. "We lost our way last night, had to sleep in the forest. They didn't like that. But," again he glanced at the bushes that bordered the track, "I gather that there was reason for them to be uneasy."

"Yes," said Brian.

"Outlaws?"

"Yes. Long Hugh and his men."

"I suppose they rob the rich and give to the poor."

"Why, no," said Brian. "They rob everyone,

rich and poor, and keep what they take for themselves."

"Very sensible," said the boy. "It's what I'd do if I were an outlaw." He dismounted. "I take it this Long Hugh is a friend of yours?"

"Let's say we have an understanding," said Brian. "But you have not told me who you are."

"I am Tertius, son of Sir Baldwin of Bedegraine."

"Tertius?"

"I have two older brothers. It means the Third."

"I know," said Brian.

"Oh? Then perhaps you can guess what my brothers' names are."

"Primus and Secundus."

"Well," said Tertius smiling, "a scholar."

"I have a little Latin," said Brian. Since he was older than Tertius, he should have been annoyed. But he was impressed, in spite of himself, by the boy's assurance and the fact that he was not only traveling alone, but carrying his own money. Besides, he liked his directness and his smile. "You come from Ferlay?"

"Yes. I have just finished my service there as page."

"You are fortunate. Sir Gerard is a brave and worthy knight."

"You did your service with him too?"

"No," said Brian somewhat awkwardly. "I have not done service, never been anywhere but Caercorbin."

"How is that?" asked Tertius. "Oh, you are an only son."

Brian nodded. "My father was killed some ten years ago fighting the paynim in the Holy Land. When word of it came to my mother, she would not let me leave. Of course Sir Guy has schooled me in the use of arms—he was my father's comrade and is now the castle steward. And Father Bernard taught me a few other things besides Latin."

"I see."

"Will you be staying with us for long?"

"No," said Tertius. "I think not."

"You would be welcome. But I suppose you are anxious to get home."

"No."

"What then?"

Instead of answering, Tertius reached inside his tunic and drew out a strange object that hung around his neck. It was round, slightly curved and made either of crystal or the clearest glass that Brian had ever seen. Holding it up, Tertius peered at him through it.

"What are you doing?" asked Brian, drawing back a little.

"It's my eyes," said Tertius. "Hyper metropia. I can see well enough at a distance, but not up close. I'd wear spectacles if they were available, but of course they're not."

"Spectacles?"

"Yes." He dropped the glass. "I think I can trust you. I'm not going home. That's why I got rid of Sir Gerard's varlets. I'm going on a quest."

Brian drew a sudden deep breath. He'd been

right then in his reading of the signs and portents, and also in his feeling that this was to be the most important day of his life so far.

"What's your friend's name, Brian?" said a voice behind him.

He and Tertius turned. Not a leaf had rustled or a twig snapped but there, on the edge of the track, stood Long Hugh and three of his men. Long Hugh was tall and lean with a short golden beard and sharp gray eves. He and his men wore deerskin jerkins. They each carried a yew bow and had half a dozen arrows thrust through their belts.

"Tertius," said Brian. "He's the son of Sir Baldwin of Bedegraine."

"Ah," said Long Hugh. "Too bad he is a friend. Pickings have been lean these past few weeks and if he had silver for those varlets, he might have had some to spare for us too."

"Since you ask me so courteously," said Tertius, reaching for his purse.

"No, no," said Long Hugh. "We try not to

trouble our friends unless our need is great. And our need today is not for silver but for something else."

"Salt again?" asked Brian.

"No. It was Hob's turn to cook and watch the fire yesterday. But when we got back to camp last night, we found that he'd slipped off to see his wife and the fire had gone out."

"Cold meat for supper," said a short, stocky outlaw. "Lucky it wasn't winter. I'll have his ears for it."

"I'll bring you some fire," said Brian. "Can you wait until vespers?"

"No need to wait," said Tertius. "I can build you a fire now."

"You?" said Long Hugh. "I had not marked you as such a seasoned traveler. You carry a flint and steel?"

"No," said Tertius. "But I have something just as good."

Tying his horse to a tree, he pushed his way through the underbrush to a clearing that lay just beyond. Brian, Long Hugh and his men followed, the outlaws exchanging grins as Tertius collected dry leaves and twigs into a small mound. Then, glancing around to find the sun, he took the glass from inside his tunic and held it so it caught the sun's rays. A bright, white spot of light appeared on the pile of leaves. They all waited a moment.

"Look 'ee, master," said the stocky outlaw. "'Tis clear you wish us well and that warms us to our umbles, but . . ."

He broke off. A wisp of smoke was curling upward from the pile of leaves and suddenly they were burning.

"Saint Michael defend me!" said Brian.

"Are you a magician?" asked Long Hugh, clutching his dagger.

"No," said Tertius, adding twigs to the fire. "At least, not yet. But if I do become one, it will be a white one. Do you have a pot for the fire?"

"No," said Long Hugh, looking at him

closely. He glanced at Brian as if for reassurance, then said, "Wat, cut a torch."

The stocky outlaw had been clutching his dagger too, holding iron to ward off evil.

"'Tis true we need fire, Hugh," he said. "But . . ."

"I give you my word it's all right," said Tertius. "It's not magic. Anyone could do it."

"Not I," said Wat. "It's unnatural." Muttering, he went over to a fir tree, cut and trimmed a branch and brought it back to Long Hugh. "Here. You do it."

Drawing his dagger, Long Hugh cut the bark on the butt end of the branch into long shavings and thrust it into the fire until it was burning briskly.

"It looks like any other fire," he said.

"It is," said Tertius.

"Well, thanks." He studied him for a moment. "I see I misjudged you in many ways."

He nodded to him and to Brian then, as suddenly and silently as they had appeared, he and his men were gone.

"There are some who would think that there was something magical about that too," said Tertius, treading out the fire. "The way they appear and disappear."

"It's only good woodcraft," said Brian. "About your quest . . ."

"Yes?"

"Does what you said about becoming a magician have anything to do with it?"

Tertius glanced at him. "You're quick," he said.

"Then it does?"

"Perhaps."

Brian sat down with his back against a tree. "Tell me," he said.

Again Tertius looked at him—a long, searching look.

"All right," he said. "I will." He sat down also. "Who was the greatest enchanter who ever lived?"

"I don't know if he was the greatest ever, but in our time . . . —Merlin?"

Tertius nodded. "He was a friend of my father's. Not that they had anything in common—all my father's ever been interested in is jousting and hunting and such. But apparently father saved his life during the fighting on Mortlake Moor, and Merlin was grateful. He not only gave him a balas ruby, but said he would be godfather to his sons."

"He knew he would have sons?"

"Yes. Father wasn't even married yet, but Merlin told him he would have three of them and what their names would be. Well, when Primus was born, father sent word to him, but Merlin never came to the christening."

"How is that?"

Tertius shrugged. "By that time he was already involved with Nimue and was traveling around the country with her. Perhaps he never got the message. But I think he forgot. Father said he always had been absentminded. He didn't come to Secundus's christening either. But he did come to mine."

"And?"

"He apparently felt bad about missing the other two christenings. Not that father cared by then because Primus and Secundus were turning out just the way he had hoped they would. But, to make up for it, Merlin worked his most potent magic and endowed me with all possible knowledge."

"Then you *are* a magician."

"No," said Tertius. "As I said, he was already infatuated with Nimue—she came to the christening with him—and he didn't have his mind on what he was doing. As a result, he made a mistake. The knowledge he endowed me with was all *future* knowledge."

"Future?"

"Yes. Do you know what a nuclear reactor is? A computer or a laser?"

"No," said Brian. "Should I?"

"Of course not. No one should for about

seven hundred years. Well, I know about them. I understand systems analysis and why the law of parity is invalid. But I can't do a simple spell to cure warts."

"And you want to?"

"I'd like to do something with what I know, something that would be useful *now*. So instead of going home, I thought I'd try and find an enchanter or magician who would take me on as an apprentice and instruct me."

"It seems a little strange for someone of gentle blood," said Brian, "someone who could be a knight. But that, then, is your quest?"

"Yes."

"It may be a long one. Merlin is gone, no one knows where. They say that, having learned his magic, Nimue used it to imprison him under a rock or in a hollow tree and that her spells were so strong he cannot free himself."

"That's true. That he's gone, I mean. But there must be others who are skilled in the same arts he was."

"Your father knows about it?"

"My quest? No. I've told no one about it before this. And I intend to tell no one else. But he won't care."

"I'm sure you do him an injustice."

"No. After all, he has Primus and Secundus. They're a pair of great lumps who can barely write their names, but they're as keen on hunting and tournaments as he is—which I'm not. As a result, father's always been uncomfortable with me. I doubt if he'll even wonder where I am."

"I find that hard to believe. But if you've told no one else about your quest, why did you tell me?"

"Because you asked me."

"I don't think that's the only reason," said Brian slowly. "You may not be skilled as yet in the magical arts, but I think you knew what was in my mind."

"Did I?"

"Yes. And you're right. I'm going with you."

Somehow Tertius did not seem surprised.

"You asked me about my father," he said. "What about your mother?"

"For years now she's asked me to wait and be patient, told me that when the time came she'd let me go. Well, today's my birthday. I'm sixteen, and I think the time has come. And so . . . I suppose I really should ask you if you'd like me to go with you."

"Why?" asked Tertius, smiling. "You read what was in my mind as easily as I read what was in yours."

"Then the answer is yes?"

"Of course. I suspect that what you'd really like is a quest of your own—one that involves a beautiful maiden and a giant, a dragon or a wicked knight. But in the meantime, mine should be interesting."

CHAPTER TWO

"I BELIEVE," SAID the Lady Leolie, "that we are distantly connected."

"I believe we are, madam," said Tertius. "On my mother's side."

The Lady Leolie, with Sir Guy beside her, had been at the high table in the great hall when Brian brought Tertius in. Brian noticed that she was wearing her hennin and her second-best dress, the green one, which meant that one of the lookouts had seen them coming and sent word to her that they had a guest. If she was surprised that that guest was so young, she gave no sign of it but welcomed Tertius as warmly as she would anyone of gentle blood.

She sat him next to her and waited patiently while he and Brian ate. Because it was Brian's birthday, or perhaps because she suspected that Tertius had had no supper the night before—she had an instinct for such things—she had game pies brought to them for breakfast instead of the usual bread and cheese.

"How's your father?" asked Sir Guy abruptly.

"I haven't seen him for some time," said Tertius. "Not since I began my service at Ferlay. But at last report he was well."

"Does he still favor his right leg, ride with his right stirrup longer than his left?"

"I believe he does."

"You should notice such things," said Sir Guy. "Very important in jousting. He's bound to favor it, especially in damp weather. I was with him when he broke it, you know. It was in the same skirmish in which I lost this." He touched the black patch that covered his missing eye. "But," glancing sideways, "that was a small loss compared to others we suffered then."

"If you are speaking of Sir Owaine," said the Lady Leolie, "he was a true and valiant knight and died a knightly death."

"That he did, my lady," said Sir Guy. "Had it not been for him, there were few of us who would have left the field that day."

Brian felt the same pang he always felt when anyone talked about his father. At first he had wondered how they could be certain he was truly dead when his body had never been found nor any ransom asked for him. He had had visions of his riding home one day with a stirring tale of his escape from his Saracen captors. But as the years went by, he had come to realize that what he had been cherishing was a child's hope. That one of the reasons he found it so hard to accept the truth was the fact that it was the loss of his father that kept him at Caercorbin.

"I have heard both my father and Sir Gerard talk of it," said Tertius politely. "Of Sir Owaine's stand and of how the fighting went. It must have been a fine melee."

"One of the best," said Sir Guy. "By the way, my squire tells me that you were alone when you arrived here."

"Sir Gerard sent a pair of varlets to ride here with me," said Tertius. "But I let them return when I met Brian."

"Ah," said Sir Guy. "Didn't sound like Sir Gerard to let you travel unaccompanied."

"Naturally we hope you'll stay with us for some time," said the Lady Leolie. "Guests are always welcome, and we are anxious to hear all the news from Ferlay. But I am sure that when you leave Sir Guy can spare you some men to see you safely home."

"You are very kind, my lady," said Tertius cautiously. "Actually, I thought of going tomorrow. But there's no need to send anyone with me."

"Nonsense," said Sir Guy. "The forest's a dangerous place—outlaws and all that. I wouldn't dream of letting you go on alone."

"Well . . ." began Tertius.

Brian swallowed. Now was the time. It was going to be difficult, but it wouldn't be easier if he waited.

"In the first place," he said, "he's not going home. He's going on a quest. And in the second place, he won't be alone because I'm going with him."

The Lady Leolie sat up stiffly.

"What did you say?"

"I said he's not going home. He's going on a quest. And I'm going with him."

The Lady Leolie shrieked, shrilly and piercingly.

"Mother!" said Brian.

The Lady Leolie shrieked again. Then her eyes rolled up, and she sank back limply in her chair.

"My lady!" said Sir Guy. "Agnes, quick!"

But Agnes was already hurrying toward them. Taking a phial of gillyflower water from her pouch, she sprinkled it on the Lady Leolie's face.

"There, there, my dearie, my duck," she said, chafing the Lady Leolie's wrists. "For shame," she said, glaring at Brian. "What did you say to set her aswooning that way?"

"Nothing," said Brian uncomfortably. "Mother, forgive me."

"Then don't ever say anything like that again!" said the Lady Leolie, opening her eyes.

"But I must," said Brian. "You always said that when the time came, you would let me go."

"Because you pressed me! But it will be years before you'll be old enough. You're still only a boy!"

"If you've forgotten, today is my birthday."

"Your sixteenth! Does that make you a man?"

"Perhaps not. But I'm no longer a boy either. Besides I've given my word to Tertius."

"Your word! What about your duty to me, your mother? I've already lost my husband. Must I now lose you, too?"

"If you will forgive me for saying so, my

lady," said Tertius mildly, "the way to keep him is to let him go."

"I want none of your logic-chopping!" she snapped. "Sir Guy . . . !"

"Fear not, my lady," he said. "If you do not wish him to go, he shall not go."

"But I am going, Sir Guy."

"You forget yourself, sirrah!" said Sir Guy, his long mustachios bristling and his single eye flashing. "While I am steward of this castle you and all others shall do my lady's bidding!"

Hardly aware of it, they were now both speaking formally, in the High Language of Chivalry.

"In all other things I am hers—and yours—to command, Sir Guy. But in this . . ."

"Do you defy me, then?"

"If it be needful to preserve my honor and my plighted word." Then a thought came to him. "No, Sir Guy. But I ask leave to prove with my body—and upon yours—that I am a boy no longer, but man enough to go."

Sir Guy was sitting very erect.

"You are challenging me?"

"Yes, Sir Guy."

"You are not a knight. I am under no obligation to accept your challenge."

"No, Sir Guy. But because *you* are a knight—and a gracious and worthy one—it is my hope that you will condescend to put the matter to the arbitrament of arms and break a spear with me."

"Speak more clearly. Precisely what is in your mind?"

"We shall joust. If you overthrow me, I shall stay here for another year. If I overthrow you, you shall let me go now."

"Ah," said Sir Guy, a strange look in his eye. "Yes."

"Sir Guy . . ." said the Lady Leolie anxiously.

"It takes many a knock to make a knight, my lady," said Sir Guy. "Let him learn now that it will be a long while before he is ready to go out into the world." Then, to Brian, "I will meet you in the tiltyard at noon."

He and the Lady Leolie rose.

"I thank you for your courtesy," said Brian, rising also.

Sir Guy answered his bow with a nod and followed the Lady Leolie out of the hall.

"Now you've done it," said Tertius.

"I suppose I have," said Brian. "I didn't mean to. I hadn't thought of it before—challenging Sir Guy, I mean. It just came out."

"Well, I don't know how far you would have gotten arguing with them . . ."

"Nowhere," said Brian. "At least, not with mother."

"But you could have tried again in a few days. This way there'll be nothing you can do for another year." He sighed. "I'm afraid you trapped yourself. Too bad. It would have been very pleasant to have had you with me."

The tiltyard was in the outer ward with the outside bailey wall on one side of it and the wall of the inner shell keep on the other; a stretch of turf open at both ends and packed hard by years of use. For it was here that pages and squires had learned to use their weapons ever since the castle had been built.

The sun was directly overhead when Brian came out of the armory door into it. Tertius had acted as his squire, helping him into the old hauberk of his father's that he had often worn during practice, raising the chain mail coif over his head, placing the arming cap on it and lacing on his tilting helm. The hauberk was a little large for him, but not enough to be awkward.

Sir Guy was already waiting at the far end of the tiltyard, mounted on Gaillard, his white charger. Simon came toward Brian, leading his own bay gelding and carrying a lance.

"You will ride my horse," said Simon, handing him the reins. "And Sir Guy said to tell you that he will be using a short spear, the same length as yours."

These were two of the many things that

Brian had been wondering about: whether he would be given a charger to ride, a horse accustomed to jousting, and what length lance Sir Guy would be carrying. For there was of course a decided advantage in a long lance. And, since Sir Guy was stronger and more experienced than Brian, he could—if he chose—use a longer one than Brian could handle at the moment.

Enclosed in the iron helm, Brian did not attempt to say anything, but nodded his thanks. He should have known, should have expected no less of Sir Guy. Simon waited while he mounted, then handed him the lance.

"Good luck," he said, his face impassive.

Again Brian nodded in acknowledgment, then turned the bay and walked it to the far end of the yard, opposite Sir Guy. So far it was all familiar: the smell of leather, the weight of the tilting helm on his shoulders and of the shield on his left arm; the feel of the tough ash lance in his right hand as he carried it with the point up, the butt resting on his right foot. For more than four years he had practiced here in the tilt-yard almost every day: in the heat of summer and the cold of winter. There was the quintain, the wooden Saracen mounted on a post against which he had ridden hundreds of times, learning to strike him in the middle of the forehead for, if your lance hit him off-center, he spun around and his outstretched arm dealt you a buffet that could unhorse you. There was the iron ring, suspended by a thread, that he had finally become skillful enough to pick up on his lance point. And there was the pelquintain, the stake on which he had practiced handstrokes under Sir Guy's critical eye, cutting high and low, right and left until he could barely lift his sword arm.

What was different about it was that now, for the first time, he was facing not an inanimate but a living target: a trained and seasoned warrior whose lance would be seeking Brian even as Brian drove against him. So there would be not only his own spear to be concerned about, but the shock of Sir Guy's spear as it smashed home against his shield, helmet or body.

Looking out through the narrow slit of his helm, Brian saw that Simon, with Tertius following him, had reached the center of the yard and was drawing his sword. And now, for the first time, he saw that his mother was seated on the bench set against the inner wall with Agnes beside her. Well, there was nothing strange about that. Everyone in the castle was there—the men-at-arms, the cook and undercooks, the scullions and serving wenches—watching from the open ends of the yard, the windows that overlooked it or the top of the outer wall. And the Lady Leolie had a greater stake in what was taking place there than anyone except Brian.

A stake: he smiled grimly. Tertius had been right. How could he have been foolish enough to challenge an experienced knight like Sir Guy? It was, of course, a combination of things that had led him to it: his eagerness to leave Caercorbin, his meeting with Tertius and the discovery that, young as he was, he was on a quest. But, mistake or not, the challenge had been accepted and all that Brian could do now was acquit himself as bravely as possible.

Simon was looking from him to Sir Guy to see if they were both ready, and Brian lowered the lance and couched it, tucking the butt between his body and his right arm, his right hand gripping it firmly.

Then, as Simon brought his sword down, calling, *"Laissez les aller!"* he drove in his heels and the bay went into a canter. While he had been waiting, his mouth had been dry, his muscles tense. But now, as he and Sir Guy thundered toward one another on the firm green turf, something deep within him took over. He seemed to hear Sir Guy's voice saying, as he had said so many times before, "Lightly as a feather, stoutly as an oak" and "Watch your point. Watch your point. *Become* your point!" He was not thinking. He was letting his muscles do what they had been trained to do, holding himself loose and limber, eyes on the tip of his lance.

They were almost upon each other, and through the slit of his helmet he could see Sir Guy and his huge white horse bearing down on him, looking larger than life-size. Then, clamping his legs to the bay and gripping the lance tightly with arm and hand, he concentrated—not just all his own strength, but the headlong drive of the horse as well—on the point of the lance and became one with it, as firm and unyielding as an oak branch.

There was a jarring double shock as Sir Guy's lance struck the center of his shield and his lance drove home against the upper edge of Sir Guy's shield. Braced for the impact that he thought would carry him backward off the bay, he found himself still in the saddle, his lance intact and still in his hand. He pulled in his horse and turned it. There was Gaillard, snorting and tossing his head, at the far end of the tiltyard. But Sir Guy was not on his back. He was lying, face upward and unmoving, near the center of the yard with his shattered lance beside him.

For a moment Brian stared, incredulous. Then, dropping his lance, he dismounted and hurried toward him. But, quick as he was, Simon was quicker. By the time Brian reached them, he had Sir Guy's helmet off and was raising his head. As Brian kneeled, Sir Guy opened his eye, looked at Brian and then past him. Brian turned. There stood the Lady Leolie, her face expressionless.

"Are you hurt?" she asked.

"No, my lady," said Sir Guy. "Stunned for a moment, that's all."

"Too bad," she said, and now she was white with rage. "I hoped you had broken your neck. Because you did that on purpose—you know you did!"

"My lady, I give you my word. . . ."

"You would tell me that a green and untried boy could unhorse you? A fig for your word!"

And, eyes blazing, she stalked off, out of the yard and into the castle.

"Is it true, Sir Guy?" asked Brian. "I mean . . ."

"That I did it on purpose? No. She's right in that I thought of it—I admit that. And I doubt if you could do it again. But it was done fairly and featly. Which, for my pride's sake, proves that I taught you even better than I knew. And now, give me your hand. For if you're to leave here tomorrow, there's much to be done and many things that we must talk about."

Holding out his hand, Brian helped Sir Guy to his feet. As he reached up to take off his own helm, it was taken off for him. Tertius was still acting as his squire. But he did not look solemn now. Poised and restrained though he was, he was grinning a wide, happy grin.

CHAPTER THREE

SUPPER THAT EVENING was a silent meal. At least, it began that way. The Lady Leolie had kept to her room most of the afternoon; and when she came down to take her place at the high table, her face was expressionless, though very pale.

The meal itself was more lavish than usual. After the fish—both trout and carp—there was a roast goose and a rack of pork as well as the joint. But of all those at the high table, only Father Bernard showed any great interest in what was put before them. The Lady Leolie was still too angry—and too distressed—to have any appetite. Brian was too disturbed at her distress and, at the same time, too excited.

And both Sir Guy and Tertius seemed to have other things on their minds.

Dinner was nearly over before the Lady Leolie broke the silence of the meal. "What is this quest upon which my son is so determined to accompany you?"

Brian was amused, wondering how Tertius was going to handle this. For obviously he wasn't going to tell her.

"I'm sorry, my lady," said Tertius, "but I'm afraid I cannot say."

"Why not?"

"It's quite proper, my lady," said Sir Guy. "King Pellinore almost never talked about the Beast Glatisant when he was hunting for it. And during the quest for the Holy Grail, most knights would not discuss their mission."

"But he's not a knight. He's not even a squire! He probably won't talk about it because it's too dangerous."

"No, my lady, it's not," said Tertius. "And that's not the reason."

"Then why . . . ?"

"Does it have anything to do with learning?" asked Father Bernard, who interested himself in such things.

"Why, yes, Father," said Tertius. "As a matter of fact, it does."

"Then there can't possibly be either harm or danger in it," said Father Bernard, "and I think we should permit the boy his secret."

"It's very clear that you're all against me," said the Lady Leolie bitterly. "All of you!"

"Mother . . ." said Brian.

"That's not true, my lady," said Sir Guy.

"It *is* true," she said. "But since there is nothing I can do about his going, thanks to you, I don't suppose it matters. Nothing today has gone the way I thought it would," she said to Brian. "But it's still your birthday. And so . . ."

She jerked her head at Agnes who brought her a large bundle.

"Here," she said, giving him a hooded traveling cloak of gray wool, "this will keep you warm. And this," giving him a purse, "will see that you do not go hungry."

"Thank you, my lady," said Brian, touched. Then he saw that she was holding something else, a shield with the Caercorbin blazon on it: a red wivern rampant on a white field.

"You will need this, too," she said. "Bear it as your father would have had you bear it."

"Mother, I will," he said. And bending down, he kissed her cheek.

"No sentimentality, please," she said, flushing slightly. "I have something else for you that I will give you in the morning. I take it that Sir Guy is seeing to it that you are properly armed."

"Yes, my lady," said Sir Guy. "He will be wearing Sir Owaine's hauberk. The armorer has been working on it all afternoon. As for weapons . . ."

Simon came forward with a sword, and Sir Guy took it from him, saying, "If your father were here, he would be giving you this as he would have given you your shield. But since he is not . . . Do you swear to draw this sword only in a just cause and to use it honorably?"

"I do."

He remained still while Sir Guy buckled it about his waist.

"Since time is short," said Sir Guy, "we have dispensed with much of the ceremony. But you understand that, having been given your own weapons, you are now an armiger and may thus take part in combat."

"Yes, Sir Guy."

Without being aware of it, Brian's hand had gone to the sword hilt and, noticing this, Sir Guy said, "You may try it if you like."

Brian drew the sword from its sheath of Cordovan leather. The hilt was bound with gold wire and fit his hand well; the whole seemed perfectly balanced.

"It is as beautiful a sword as I have ever seen," he said.

"It's a good blade," said Sir Guy. "I had it from a Spanish knight whom I overthrew at a tourney in France. May it serve you well."

"Thank you, Sir Guy," said Brian, greatly moved. "I do not know what else I can say except . . ."

"Then say nothing. I too will have something else for you in the morning. And now, be off with you."

"But . . ."

"Do you mean to get an early start?"

"Yes, Sir Guy."

"Then off with you, both of you!"

Wordlessly, Brian reached for Sir Guy's hand, pressed it warmly, then he and Tertius left the great hall.

They did not get as early a start as they had planned. Brian was too excited to sleep, as he had been too excited to eat; and he and Tertius stayed up until late talking. Even after Tertius fell asleep, Brian lay in the dark of the tower room, thinking of all that had happened that day—of his new friend, his new freedom and his new sword—and of what might lie ahead.

When Brian and Tertius came down in the morning, much later than they had intended, they found that the armorer had still not finished his work on the hauberk. He was an old man, gray as a badger. He had seen to Sir Owaine's arms before the journey to the Holy Land, and he was not to be hurried, even by Sir Guy. He would not give Brian the hauberk until he had replaced every doubtful link in the chain mail and was completely satisfied with it.

And so it was nearly noon when Brian and Tertius went out into the courtyard where the Lady Leolie and Sir Guy waited for them. Tertius' gray palfrey saddled and ready, stood near the entrance to the great hall and next to him, tossing his head impatiently, was—not Mab, the chestnut mare Brian had ridden for years—but Gaillard, Sir Guy's white charger.

"What's this?" asked Brian surprised.

"I said I had something else for you," said Sir Guy gruffly. "After all, you can't go off on a quest riding a twelve-year-old mare."

"You're giving me Gaillard? But you can't!"

"Are you telling me what I can do and what I can't?"

"No, Sir Guy."

"Then be silent!"

For a moment Brian looked at Sir Guy and Sir Guy looked at him, his single eye proud and fierce. Then, as he had the night before, Brian took his hand.

"Thank you, Sir Guy," he said simply. "I will tend him well."

"If I did not think you would, I would not be giving him to you. Remember that, if anything, he is overeager. If you should happen to joust again—and I hope you will not—hold him back until the last moment, then give him his head."

"I'll remember," said Brian.

He turned now to his mother. She was dressed as she had been the day before, in her good green gown, and, her face, though it was still pale, was composed.

"I, too, said I had something else for you," she said. "Here." And she took off a heavy gold ring and gave it to him.

"Your ring?"

"It is not my ring. It is the Caercorbin ring, one of a pair. Your father had one exactly like it. He wore it when he went off to the Holy Land. It is only right that you wear its companion."

Brian looked at it, though he did not need to, for he had admired it for as long as he could remember. As his mother said, it was the Caercorbin ring, for it was made in the likeness of a wivern, their blazon, but cunningly wrought so that the winged dragon held his tail in his teeth, thus making a circle.

Brian glanced at his mother, then slipped it on the little finger of his left hand.

"Very well, Mother."

"God and Saint Michael guard you," she said. "And," almost whispering, "come back!"

"Fear not, Mother," he said, embracing her, "I will."

Then, afraid to trust himself to say more, he swung up onto Gaillard. Simon, standing beside Sir Guy, handed him a lance. Tertius was already in the saddle, and together they moved toward the gatehouse. When they were under the portcullis, Brian turned and looked back. There in the center of the courtyard—exactly as he had seen them in his dream—stood his mother and Sir Guy, watching them go: his mother holding herself tall and straight and with only a faint mistiness in her blue eyes.

It was too much. Driving his heels into Gaillard, Brian sent him thundering across the drawbridge, the open space beyond and into the leafy shade of the forest. Struggling with his own feelings, he gave the great white horse his head and they galloped along the forest track, Brian holding his lance low to avoid the overhanging branches. Finally, coming to a place where the narrow road curved slightly to the east, he checked Gaillard. A few minutes later Tertius came cantering up.

"We have a long way to go," he said reprovingly, "and we'll never get there if we start out this way."

"I know. I'm sorry."

"It's all right." Then, looking closely at Brian, "Are *you* all right?"

"Yes."

"Good."

They started up the track at an easier pace, riding side by side.

"By the way, exactly where are we going?" asked Brian.

"I don't know."

"But we are looking for an enchanter?"

"Yes. I'd thought of trying Master Blaise. He was Merlin's teacher. But I understand he's no longer up in Northumberland. It's said that he's now in France."

"Shall we go there then?"

"Perhaps. But there must be other magicians who are closer to home."

"I'm sure there are. You were wise not to

tell my mother what your quest was. I don't think she would have liked it."

"Neither would Father Bernard. But I didn't tell an untruth. After all, it does have something to do with learning."

"Not what he would call learning."

"No. Though of course chemistry grew out of alchemy. And I suspect that magic isn't what we think. Or," suddenly thoughtful, "perhaps that's the answer. Perhaps that's exactly what it is."

"What what is?"

"Magic."

"Everyone knows what magic is."

"Really? What is it, then?"

"Why, magic. The only question is whether it's black or white."

"And how can you tell the difference?"

"I suppose it depends on whether it's good or bad, whether it helps people or hurts them. Merlin was a white magician. He used his magic to help people."

"But you believe in both kinds?"

"Of course."

Tertius nodded, still looking thoughtful. And so they rode on, sometimes talking, but often silent. They met no one during the long afternoon, but they had no trouble following the tree-shaded track until the sun was low in the west. Then they came to a place where the road forked, one branch going south and one east.

"Which way?" asked Brian, reining in Gaillard.

"I've no idea," said Tertius.

"It all depends on where you want to go," said a familiar voice.

They turned. As before, Long Hugh had appeared out of nowhere and was standing by the side of the track, leaning on his bow.

"You're a long way from home," said Brian.

"How can that be when the whole forest is my home?"

"Well, from Caercorbin, then."

"For you, perhaps, by road. Not so far for me by forest paths."

"We are well-met," said Tertius. "Where do these roads go?"

"This one," said Hugh, pointing to the right, "will take you home to Bedegraine. The other will take you to Meliot."

"Then the choice is easy," said Tertius. "We go straight ahead."

"To Meliot?"

"Yes."

"You will not get there before dark when the gates close. I think you had better spend the night with us."

"Your camp is near here?" asked Brian.

"One of our camps."

"We would like that, Hugh," said Brian. "Thank you."

"It is not far. You had better lead your horses."

Brian and Tertius dismounted and followed him. They had barely left the track when they discovered why he had told them to lead their horses; the undergrowth was so thick and the branches hung so low that a mounted man could not have gone more than a few paces without being swept from the saddle. On they went, turning and twisting to avoid boggy places and patches of briars, until they came out into a stand of oaks.

As they started through it, a pair of partridges rose to their left and flew fast and low for cover. With almost unbelievable speed, Hugh whipped an arrow from his belt, nocked it, drew and loosed. While it was still in the air, he had drawn and loosed another. Both birds fell, each spitted by a clothyard shaft.

Brian whistled softly with admiration and Hugh nodded.

"Fair shooting," he admitted. "But when your life depends on your bow—for food or defense—you learn to use it."

"I can use one," said Brian. "But I doubt that I could ever learn to shoot like that."

"It's not a gentle's weapon," said Hugh. "I misdoubt that I could ever learn to use that spear of yours."

He had picked up the two birds and was leading them on. A short distance beyond the oaks, they came to an open glade. A fire burned in its center and set about it were crude but snug shelters roofed with pine boughs. Half a dozen men lounged about the fire on which a haunch of venison was roasting, among them Wat, the stocky outlaw. The man tending the fire had a black eye and, when Wat saw Brian and Tertius looking at him, he nodded.

"Aye," he said, "that's our wandering Hob. I left him his ears but thought a buffet might remind him that we each have our duties."

"Next time you try to remind me of anything," growled Hob, "I'll use six inches of steel to remind you to keep your hands to yourself."

"No more of that," said Hugh firmly. "When outlaws fall out with one another, their plight is bad indeed."

"Well, perhaps I deserved the buffet," said Hob. "But I don't like having it talked about. Is this the young wizard who drew fire from the sun for you?"

"It is," said Hugh. "So burn the roast, and he'll scorch your hide."

"He doesn't look so wizardlike to me," said Hob. "Nor vengeful either."

"But I am hungry," said Tertius.

"Ah, that's something else again," said Hob. "Tend to your horses, young masters; and by the time you've done that, I'll have as tasty a supper ready for you as was ever eaten in the greenwood."

He may have been lacking as a fire watcher, but he was a reliable cook. Brian and Tertius unsaddled their horses, rubbed them down and set them to grazing. When they came back to the fire, the venison was done and served to them with horns of mead. Afterward, as it grew dark and they sat around the glowing logs, they had honeycomb, which one of the outlaws had taken from a wild bee's tree only that morning.

Brian waited for Hugh to question him about why he had left Caercorbin and where he was going. But forest men never pry into the affairs of others, wanting no one to pry into theirs. And so the talk was only about the movement of game and why wild boars were so scarce and deer so plentiful and whether Long Hugh and some of the others should go north and take part in a shooting match in which the prize was to be a silver arrow.

Later, Brian and Tertius stretched out in one of the shelters and, as they looked up at the clear summer sky, Brian said, "When you learn magic will you also learn the stars?"

"I already know them."

"I don't mean their names and positions. I mean, will you learn to read them?"

"There are," said Tertius, "some several dozen so-called methods of divination. For instance, *crystallomancy*, which is gazing into crystals, *pyromancy,* which is studying fire, *capnomancy,* which involves smoke, *hydromancy,* which involves water, *cleromancy,* which makes use of dice, *alectryomancy, oneiromancy, chiromancy, stichomancy.* Shall I go on?"

"No," said Brian. "And they are all true?"

"They are all nonsense."

"But if that's so, then why do people believe in them?"

"People believe in a great many ridiculous things. That the earth is flat, for instance."

Brian lifted himself on one elbow. "You mean it's not?"

"No."

"But you can see that it is."

"Can you?"

"Of course." Then, "If it's not flat, what is it?"

"Let's not go into that now."

"Why not?"

"Because it's too complicated."

Brian looked down at him, frowning. The

things that Tertius seemed to know—the things he said with such assurance—may have been the result of a mistake of Merlin's, but Brian couldn't help wondering if he himself wasn't making a mistake, imperiling his immortal soul, by consorting with him. For much of what he said, and some of what he did, was not merely strange, but bordered on the heretical. Tertius returned his glance calmly, and Brian had a feeling that, in a sense, this was a test. That if he accepted this last statement of his that the earth was not flat, he would accept anything Tertius said or did.

"All right," he said. "But the stars are different. There are so many of them, each with its own properties and each acting upon us for good or evil. There must be something to the reading of them."

While they were arguing about it, they fell asleep.

CHAPTER FOUR

LONG HUGH PAUSED where the trees ended and the ground became more open.

"The road is just beyond the hedgerow," he said.

Brian and Tertius had awakened early that morning, but not as early as their hosts. By the time they had washed in the brook near the camp, all the outlaws except Hugh and Hob had disappeared into the greenwood, some to hunt, some to keep watch for any who might be searching for them. After breakfasting on the partridges that Hugh had shot the day before, they said good-bye to Hob and followed Hugh along narrow and almost invisible trails to the edge of the forest.

"How far is it to Meliot?" asked Brian.

"Perhaps three miles," said Hugh. "But since there are many hereabouts who know me, I will come no further with you."

"We thank you for your hospitality," said Brian.

"It was a small return for past favors," said Hugh. "I'm still in your debt. And," to Tertius, "perhaps in yours, too."

"For the fire? That was nothing."

"Since we needed it, it was a great deal. But that was not what I meant. When we first met, I told you that the pickings near Caercorbin had been slim. And so, for some time before that, we had been ranging further south."

"To Bedegraine?"

"Thereabouts."

"And did you do better there?" asked Tertius, smiling.

"Much better. The roads are more traveled

in those parts, and those who travel them had more to share with us."

"I see," said Tertius. "Well, I'm sure you took no more than you needed or than the travelers could spare."

"It always seemed to me that we were fair," said Hugh. "But you'd be surprised at how opinions differ on such things."

"What about my brothers?" asked Tertius. "Had you any trouble with them? I would have thought that hunting outlaws would be very much to their taste."

"The word was that they had gone off somewhere. And perhaps it was just as well. For hunting outlaws can be a dangerous sport."

"I can well imagine that," said Tertius, looking at the arrows in Hugh's belt. "But since what happens at Bedegraine has little to do with me, I still consider that we are friends."

"Good," said Hugh. "I can use friends more than most men. And so, a good journey to you. Or rather, a good quest." And raising his hand in farewell, he disappeared into the forest.

"How did he know we were on a quest?" asked Brian. "Did you tell him?"

"No," said Tertius. "But sharp wits go with sharp ears and eyes. I think he is someone who will always know more than he seems to. Shall we ride?"

They mounted and almost at once Gaillard, tired of restraint and eager for exercise, broke into a canter. Tertius's gray followed, and so they raced over the meadows and soon gained the road. It was wide, white, and dusty; and for the first time since leaving Caercorbin, they began to encounter other travelers. There were country folk in carts, some drawn by horses and some by oxen, chapmen on slow-pacing hacks leading sumpter mules, pilgrims with silver badges on their hats and staves in their hands, and farmers and their wives. They were all moving in the same direction, east toward Meliot. And as Brian and Tertius turned their horses that way, many eyes followed them—

particularly those of the women—for, though Brian did not know it, he made a brave sight as he guided Gaillard up the road, the sun bright on his flaxen hair and newly burnished hauberk.

Reaching the top of a hill, they paused for a moment, for there below them was Meliot. It was a fair town, set in rich farmland with a wide river just beyond it. On the far side of the river there was a forest as thick and dark as the one they had just left, but on the near side all was open, green with pasture and golden with growing grain. A high wall circled the town, and at intervals, strengthening the wall, there were round towers pierced by arrow slits. The road went down the hill and through the wide open gates and, following it, Brian and Tertius found themselves in narrow, cobbled streets where the houses jutted out so that they almost touched overhead. Even when they came to the merchants' quarter where the street was wider, the throng was so thick that they could barely press their way through it and finally, opposite a goldsmith's shop, they dismounted.

The goldsmith, a portly man with a forked beard and shrewd eyes, was standing in the doorway.

"Is your town always like this?" Brian asked him. "Or is this a Fair day?"

"There are some who may treat it as a Fair day," he said, "but it is not. It is Midsummer Day, which is one of the two darkest days of the year for Meliot. For it is tribute day."

"Tribute?" Looking more closely at those who were passing by, Brian noticed for the first time that none of them looked gay and excited as they would if they were going to a fair, but sober and serious. "To whom do you pay tribute?"

"To the Black Knight of Benoye," said the goldsmith. "You must have come from faraway if you have not heard the tale."

"We come from far enough so that we have not," said Brian. "But we would like to hear it."

"It is a grim tale," said the goldsmith, settling

himself against the doorpost. "It began some score of years ago. Until that time Meliot had been a rich and happy town. We had some of the most prosperous merchants, the best weavers, gold and silversmiths in all Britain. Early each summer they would journey in company across the ford and through the forest, south to Camelot and east to London, to sell their wares, returning again in the fall. Then, in the reign of King Rience, that all changed."

"How?" asked Brian.

"One day, when they arrived at the ford to begin their journey, they found a knight in black armor there. No one knew who he was, but it was said that he had traveled in the East and learned dark arts. He told the merchants that no knight could cross the river unless he jousted with him and no merchant should cross unless he paid him a tenth of all his goods as a toll."

"Was he alone?" asked Tertius.

"No. He had more than a hundred men-at-arms with him. Well, the merchants returned and told the king about it. Rience was a famous jouster; so he armed himself and rode down to the ford, and he and the Black Knight had at one another."

"And?"

"The Black Knight overthrew him, giving him such a great fall that for several days he lay unconscious. Now King Rience had two sons, Dinas and Galleron, and they were skilled jousters, too. When King Rience was himself again, Dinas, the elder son, armed himself and went against the Black Knight, and the Black Knight overthrew him as he had the king. The fall that he gave him was so great that Dinas never recovered from the hurt and some time later he died."

"You said it was a grim tale," said Brian. "And it is."

"It becomes even more so. By now it was almost midsummer, and the merchants came to the king and pressed him to win them passage of the ford. For if they were delayed much longer, they would not be able to complete their journeys and return before the bad weather set in. The king, heartsick at the death of Sir Dinas, swore a great oath, saying, 'I swear by my head that I shall deal with this Black Knight!' Hearing this, Galleron, his youngest son, begged that he might go against him, and Rience finally agreed. But he did not let him go alone. Rience followed him with a company of bowmen."

"Bowmen?" said Brian, frowning.

"Yes," said the goldsmith. "Galleron and the Black Knight met at the ford. And when Galleron was overthrown like his father and his brother, King Rience signaled his archers. They loosed a flight of arrows, and the Black Knight fell into the river and did not rise again."

"Wicked though the Black Knight may have been," said Brian, "that was still an evil deed."

"It was," agreed the goldsmith. "He was an honorable man, was King Rience, and he would never have done it if he had not lost his son and if the merchants had not pressed him so hard. But he paid for it. And we have been paying for it ever since."

"How so?"

"In the morning the merchants gathered again and prepared to leave on their journey through the forest. But when they reached the ford there, as before, was the Black Knight, waiting for them."

"But he was dead," said Brian. "You said that he fell into the river and did not rise again."

"If he were a mortal man, he would have been dead," said the goldsmith. "He was struck by more than a score of arrows. But I also said that he had learned dark arts in the East. The merchants hurried back to Meliot and told the king what had happened. And hard on their heels, into the town square, came the Black Knight and his men."

"They came into the town?"

"Yes. The Black Knight rode up to Rience

and said, 'I am here for the fulfillment of your oath, oh king.' 'What oath?' asked Rience. 'You swore by your head that you would deal with me,' said the Black Knight. 'But, as you see, you did not. So I am here for your head.' And he drew his sword."

Several passersby had stopped while the goldsmith was telling this tale. And, though it was one they all must have known, they sighed.

"And did he . . . ?" asked Brian.

"No," said the goldsmith. "Rience had always been a good king, and one of the merchants, a friend of my father's, began to reason with the Black Knight, offering him the weight of the king's head in gold if he would let him live. At first the Black Knight refused. But the merchant increased the offer and finally he made one that was acceptable. The Black Knight would come here twice a year, on Midsummer Day and at Yule, and issue a challenge. If no one answered it and overcame him, he would be given the weight of the king's head in gold. In addition, the merchants who wished to travel through the forest would pay him a tithe of the value of their goods."

Again those who stood listening behind Brian and Tertius sighed.

"What they had agreed to was written out by a clerk and signed," said the goldsmith. "The king and the merchants each put up one half of the gold, and the next day the merchants left for their journey through the forest, each paying out the tenth part of the value of their goods. At Yule the Black Knight came again, and they paid him his tribute, and again the next midsummer. But this time some of the merchants who made the journey did not come back. For, they said to themselves, why should we pay part of our goods to the Black Knight and also give gold for tribute when he can live freely in London, Camelot or one of the other towns? And so it has been ever since. Each year there are more who do not come back, and year by year Meliot has become less and less, until now it is but a shadow of what it once was."

Looking again at those who filled the street, Brian saw that most of them were not townspeople, but folk from the surrounding countryside. And he also saw that many of the shops nearby were empty and the houses boarded up.

"This has been going on for how long?" asked Tertius.

"Since my father's time," said the goldsmith. "For more than twenty years now."

"And there has been no one in all that time to challenge the Black Knight?" asked Brian.

"There have been many," said the goldsmith. "Especially in the beginning. During the first few years, champions came from all over Britain to break a spear with the Black Knight. But he overcame them all, killing many of them. And during these past few years there have been fewer and fewer who have even dared to try him."

"And this has been going on for more than twenty years?" said Tertius.

"You are thinking that in that time he must have grown older and his strength less," said the goldsmith. "That would be true if he were a mortal man. But it is clear that he is not."

"Why so?" asked Tertius.

"Because he was not slain by that storm of arrows and because he is still as strong and dangerous as ever. Rience died a few years after it all began. Of grief for Dinas, we think, and because of the woe that had come on Meliot. And his younger son, Galleron, became king. Some time after that, after many stout champions had gone against the Black Knight to no avail, King Galleron sent a messenger to Merlin, asking him what could be done about it. And Merlin sent back word that, in all the world, there was only one knight who could overthrow the Black Knight. And that was the Knight with the Red Shield."

"Who is he, this Knight with the Red Shield?" asked Brian.

"No one knows," said the goldsmith. "And

of course ever since then there have been few who have dared answer the Black Knight's challenge. For they feel there is no hope of conquering him."

"Has anyone ever seen his face, this Black Knight of yours?" asked Tertius.

"Why, no," said the goldsmith. "At least, no one but his own men. For he comes here fully armed, with his helmet on. Why do you ask?"

"I just wondered," said Tertius.

"I'm not a fearful man," said the goldsmith, "but I do not think I would like to see his face."

"When does he come here?" asked Brian.

"Very soon now, at high noon," said the goldsmith. "If you would see him, go up this street to the town square. For that is where he will confront the king."

"Thank you," said Brian. "And thank you for telling us the tale."

"There is nothing to thank me for. It is a tale that anyone in the shire could have told you."

"Before we go," said Tertius, "can you, by any chance, cut and polish gems?"

"Yes, I can," said the goldsmith, glancing at him with sudden interest. "I learned the art in the Low Countries where they are more skilled at it than anywhere else. Why? Do you have a gem you wished cut?"

"Not exactly a gem," said Tertius. Then, seeing Brian's impatience, "This won't take long, Brian. But if you don't want to wait, go ahead and I'll meet you in the square."

"I'll save a place for you," said Brian. And leading Gaillard, he joined the crowd that was moving slowly up the narrow street.

CHAPTER FIVE

THE PRESS BECAME even thicker as Brian went up the street; and Gaillard became restive, for he was not used to crowds. Coming to an inn, Brian led him into the yard and, turning him over to a stableboy, went on his way on foot.

The town square was just a few paces from the inn, and it was so large that even with those who had been coming in from the countryside all morning, it was still not full. Standing next to an elderly yeoman in a homespun tunic, Brian looked around. And now, having heard the tale of Meliot's plight, he could see signs of decay everywhere. Grass grew between the cobblestones that paved the square, and there were empty shops and boarded-up houses. And of those that were still lived in, many were in bad repair: their plaster facing cracked and weatherbeaten and their shutters broken or hanging crookedly.

Opposite Brian was a church, and on the steps there was a throne with a faldstool on either side of it. Seeing him looking at it, the yeoman said, "Aye. That is where the king will sit when he comes out of the church."

"And the stools?"

"They are for his daughters."

"I did not know he had daughters."

"He has two of them."

"But there are only two stools. What about the queen?"

"She is dead. She died soon after the princesses were born."

"Your king is a man who has had many misfortunes."

"That he has. And so have we all. Year by year things go harder with us."

"Because of the tribute?"

"Because of the tribute and because each year there are fewer here in Meliot to whom we, who hold land, can sell what we raise. Twice a year I come here, as do all these others, hoping each time that some champion will have heard of the evil that has been visited on us, take up the Black Knight's challenge and break his hold on us."

"But haven't many tried to do so?"

"Not in recent years. There was one who tried this past Yule, a Sir Uriel, but the Black Knight made short shrift of him. Of course," he looked shrewdly at Brian, "now that the princesses are of a marriageable age perhaps things will be different."

"Perhaps. What about today? Is there anyone . . . ?"

"I have not heard of anyone. Certainly not the Knight with the Red Shield who, they say, is the only one who can deal with him."

There was a faint murmur from the crowd and, looking across the square to the church, Brian saw that the door was opening. A priest came out and after him, King Galleron, followed by his daughters. The king was a tall man, richly dressed in a dark velvet robe of state. And though he was not old, his face was deeply lined and he was somewhat stooped as if his crown were too heavy for him. The priest remained standing by the church door, but the king came forward and seated himself on the throne, and his daughters took their places on either side of him. Seeing them, Brian had eyes for no one else.

They were about his own age, one dark and one fair. The dark one was slender with a firm chin and eyes that looked out levelly at the crowd. But the fair one was so beautiful that she took his breath away. Her hair was wheat-blond and her eyes were blue and, after a quick glance around the square, she lowered them modestly and kept them down.

"The dark one is Lianor," said Tertius, "and the fair one is Alys. They're twins."

Brian started. Staring at Alys, he had not

seen Tertius working his way through the crowd to stand beside him.

"But how can they be twins," he asked, "when one is dark and one is fair?"

"Perfectly possible. They're not identical twins. They're fraternal."

"Oh," said Brian, not understanding and not caring that he didn't. "Isn't she beautiful?"

"Which?"

Brian looked at him in astonishment. "Alys, of course."

"Why, yes. Or at least she's quite pretty, if you like that type."

"Pretty?" said Brian indignantly. "She's . . ."

He was interrupted by the sound of a horn. It was not the clear, silver call of a hunting horn, but a harsh, rasping blast that set the teeth on edge. Again the crowd murmured and began moving back, pressing close about the sides of the square and leaving the center clear. There was the slow plod of horses' hoofs, the tramp of many feet, and into the square came the Black Knight and his men.

The Black Knight rode a huge black stallion with wicked, red-rimmed eyes. His helmet was black and so was his shield and hauberk; the mail was dinted and rusty with brownish patches on it that looked like dried blood. He carried a lance and a two-handed sword hung from his belt. Behind him rode his captain, a lean, gray-bearded, hard-bitten man in a steel cap riding a rangy roan. And behind him, in ordered ranks, marched his men-at-arms, as dangerous and wolfish-looking as their captain, and like him, all wearing mail and steel caps.

Slowly, looking neither to the right nor the left, the Black Knight walked his charger across the square. Wearing a tilting helm, he was faceless. But it was his controlled slowness that made him seem even more terrible. For, moving as he did, he seemed not human, but something mechanical, driven by clockwork. Arriving in front of the king, he checked his horse, and his captain drew up alongside him, the men-at-arms forming a phalanx behind them.

"You know why we are here, O king," said the captain. "Is there anyone who challenges our right to be here or our right to our Midsummer tribute?"

The king, his face drawn, looked around the square and there was silence: no one in the close-packed crowd stirred or even seemed to breathe.

"Again I ask," said the captain, "is there anyone here who challenges our right to our tribute?"

Hardly aware of what he was doing, Brian found himself moving. Pushing past those who stood in front of him, he stepped out into the square.

"Yes," he said in a clear voice. "I challenge your right to tribute, and I challenge the Black Knight to prove that right by breaking a spear with me."

There was a gasp, a surprised murmur from the crowd. The captain turned and looked at

Brian as the king, his daughters and everyone in the vast throng were already doing. Only the Black Knight did not move, but sat his horse staring straight ahead of him.

"Who are you?" asked the captain.

"I am Brian of Caercorbin, son of Sir Owaine of Caercorbin."

"You are a knight?"

"No. I am only a squire, but I am an armiger."

"The Black Knight does not fight with boys," said the captain contemptuously.

"He shall fight with me," said Brian hotly, "or I shall proclaim him a false and recreant knight and a dastard!"

The captain looked long at him, then glanced sideways at his master. Still without turning, the Black Knight made a slight gesture.

"Very well," said the captain. "Get your horse. If you have a horse."

"I have a horse," said Brian.

The crowd parted as he strode back toward

the street that led to the inn, and now the eyes that were on him, though warm, were anxious and the murmurs were not of surprise but concern. Gaillard tossed his head and neighed in greeting when he saw him. Brian untethered him and took his gauntlets and tilting helm from his saddlebag. Then Tertius was there, his face pale.

"You're mad!" he said. "Clean out of your wits! You know that, don't you?"

"Yes," said Brian, raising the hood of his hauberk and placing his arming cap on it. "Help me with my helmet."

"This isn't Sir Guy, with whom you were far luckier than you deserved to be. This Black Knight is a killer."

"I know."

"Then why did you do it?"

"Because I had to. You heard and saw what's been happening here. I could not stand there before the whole town—a whole shire—and let his challenge go unanswered."

"You could not! What's Meliot to you? Or

was it the Princess Alys's beautiful blue eyes?"

"I had to do it!" said Brian impatiently. "I don't know why. I didn't even know I was going to until I did it. Now will you help me?"

"No," said Tertius.

"Very well. Then I'll do it myself." And putting on the helmet, he began fumbling with the thongs that held it in place.

"You know your trouble, don't you?" said Tertius. "You've read too many knightly tales, and you believe them: believe that the true knight who's pure in heart shall conquer. I suspected it when we first met and even liked you for it. But if I'd realized how deep it went! All right. Stop making a cat's cradle of those thongs. I'll do it."

Deftly he laced the helmet on. Then, when Brian had swung up into the saddle, he handed him his shield and lance.

"Thanks," said Brian.

"Don't thank me. You're making me feel like a murderer, too. If you should live through this, we'll have to have a talk. Meanwhile . . . Good luck, Brian."

"Thanks," said Brian again.

Touching his heels to Gaillard, he sent him cantering out of the innyard, up the street and into the square. A sigh greeted him and not a few people crossed themselves and murmured a prayer.

The Black Knight had not moved. He still sat his charger in the center of the square, facing the king. But when Brian appeared, he turned the stallion and, holding him on a tight rein, sent him pacing slowly to the far end of the square. Brian turned Gaillard and rode the other way, then turned again so that he was facing the Black Knight, with the whole length of the square between them.

Looking to the left through the slit in his helmet, Brian could see the king and his two daughters on the church steps. Their eyes were on him but, while Galleron and Lianor were serious, frowning, Alys's lips were parted in a small smile and her eyes were shining. He glanced to his right. The Black Knight's captain stood there, his sword drawn, prepared to act as marshall and give them the signal. Though he could see little of the crowd, he could sense it all around him.

He couched his lance. Gaillard had seen the black stallion and was tossing his head, straining to be off. And then, suddenly, exactly what it meant—the things Tertius had tried to tell him—came home to him. Though the midday sun blazed down on him from overhead, as he looked at the Black Knight, still and faceless, on the far side of the square, he began to tremble with a chill that was not physical. For it seemed to him that whoever the Black Knight was and wherever he had come from, he could not be human.

The captain raised his sword and, clenching his teeth, Brian fought to steady himself. Then, as the sword came down, he drove in his heels and Gaillard was off, pounding over the cobbles in a gallop. Now, as before, Brian's muscles took over and he rode loosely, holding Gaillard slightly in check, gripping his lance lightly but firmly. Though Simon's horse had been well-trained, strong and eager, he had never felt such controlled power as he now felt between his thighs. But the black stallion was just as big as Gaillard, perhaps even bigger. He bore down on Brian like a thundercloud in a gale, head forward, teeth bared and eyes wild. And if the Black Knight had been terrible before in his stillness, he was even more terrible now as he thundered down—at one with the stallion—like some massive engine of destruction.

They were almost upon each other. Giving Gaillard his head, Brian clamped his legs and gripped his lance tightly, driving the point at the center of the Black Knight's shield. There was a sudden tremendous shock and, as Brian's lance shattered, it was as if he had been struck by a thunderbolt. For there was a sudden blaze of light, so bright that it blinded him, then all became dark.

CHAPTER SIX

THE FIRST THING Brian saw when he opened his eyes was a canopy. Puzzled, he looked up at it, then around. The canopy was over a bed. He was lying in the bed, a much larger one than his mother's, in a completely strange room. It too was larger than his mother's and much more richly furnished. There were not only chests and benches in it, but several chairs and a table, and two of the walls were covered by tapestries.

His head ached and, when he tried to sit up, he winced at the sudden sharp pain in his right side and shoulder.

"Greetings," said Tertius, coming over to

the bed from the window. "I gather I don't have to tell you to be careful how you move."

"No," said Brian. "Where is this?"

"The castle."

"King Galleron's?"

"Yes. They brought you in here from the square. How do you feel?"

"Well, my head hurts, and my shoulder and my side, but . . ."

"It's not surprising. You've been unconscious since they brought you here. And that was yesterday."

"Yesterday?"

"Yes. I think you had a concussion. Your collarbone and several ribs were broken, and you have a great gash in your side. But you were still lucky. Not as lucky as you were with Sir Guy, but luckier than you deserved to be."

"Yes," said Brian. "I suppose I was." Looking down, he saw that his right arm was in a sling and that a bandage circled his chest. "Who's been taking care of me? You?"

"No. The princess."

"Alys?" he asked hopefully.

"No, Lianor. She seems quite good at it."

"Oh," said Brian. "Exactly what happened? I mean, I know I was unhorsed . . ."

"His lance must have glanced off your shield. The mail of your hauberk was torn on the right side. And when you fell, you got the concussion and broke your collarbone."

Brian nodded. "It was only my second joust. I'll do better next time."

"And when will that be?" asked Tertius coldly.

"I don't know. They paid the tribute?"

"Yes. It's all over until Yule."

"You're still angry at me, aren't you?"

"Not as angry as I was. I thought you were going to be killed."

"So did I. For a moment, anyway. But by that time, there was nothing I could do about it."

The door opened and King Galleron and the

Princess Lianor came in. The king's face was still drawn and careworn but, when he saw Brian sitting up, it relaxed somewhat.

"You're awake, then. I'm glad. We were concerned about you."

"There was no reason to be, Your Majesty," said Brian.

"Wasn't there? My brother, Dinas, lay in a swoon like that after fighting the Black Knight, and he never awoke from it."

"I told you this was different, father," said Lianor.

"So you did. But when a man has lived with misfortune for as long as I have, he expects the worst. Are you in much pain?" he asked Brian.

"No, Your Majesty. Only when I try to move my arm."

"Which you shouldn't do," said Lianor. "Not for some time."

"You'd best listen to her," said the king. "She's a good healer, has been ever since she was a child. She said you would be better today, but

I wanted to see that for myself. And I also wanted to thank you for what you did yesterday."

"But I did nothing, Your Majesty. Or at least I accomplished nothing."

"You tried, risked your life to help us and no one can do more than that. If I'd known that you were going to challenge the Black Knight, I would have forbidden it. For it's been said that there's only one man in the world who can overthrow him."

"The Knight with the Red Shield."

"You knew that?"

"Yes."

"And still you challenged him. Why?"

"I suppose because I didn't believe it."

The king smiled faintly. "If there's ever a time when we believe we're invincible, it's when we're young. But we all meet our Black Knights."

"Who, in turn, will one day face the Knight with the Red Shield."

"True," said the king. "At least, I hope it's true and that it happens soon. For if it does not . . ." He broke off. "But that is my concern, not yours. As I said, I came here to thank you, which I do. And since you will be staying here with us until you are well, and as long after that as you wish, we shall talk again."

Nodding to Brian and Tertius, he left. Now Lianor came over to the bed. She wore a short-sleeved yellow gown, and her dark hair hung down her back in two braids. She carried a basket in which there were flasks, vials and small earthenware jars. She set it down, and with deft, steady hands took off the bandage. Brian looked down at his side with a good deal of interest; after all, it was his first wound. Though it was long, running from his chest around to his back, it did not seem deep.

"It's healing," said Lianor. "But this will make it heal more quickly." And taking one of the jars from the basket, she spread a grayish ointment on the wound.

Tertius had come over to the bed too.

"May I ask what that is, princess?" he asked.

"An ointment."

"Yes, but what's it made of? It's not vervaine, millefoil or pennyroyal."

"If you must know, it's made of mold."

"I thought so. An antibiotic," he explained to Brian.

"No. It's just mold, mixed with a few herbs and simples." She was putting the bandage on again. "There. As for your ribs and collarbone, they should be mended in three or four weeks."

"Three or four weeks?" said Brian.

"Yes. Why do you sound so dismayed? Do you find it so unpleasant here?"

"No, princess. Of course not. It's just that Tertius and I are on a quest. . . ."

"What sort of a quest?"

"I'm afraid I can't tell you."

"I see. Well, you won't be able to use that arm for some time, so you'll just have to make the best of it."

"Yes, princess." And when she had finished putting on the bandage and adjusting the sling, "Thank you."

"There's no need to thank me. I've done as much for others who did far less for Meliot."

"Where did you learn your healing?"

"Here and there. Why?"

"It seems strange for a princess to know such things."

"No stranger than it is for anyone else. I had a nurse who was a very wise woman and she taught me."

"Your sister, too?"

She looked at him shrewdly. Her lashes were long and dark and her eyes were green, a deep sea-green, with golden lights in them.

"No. Alys was interested in other things."

"What other things?"

"If you don't know, why don't you ask her?"

Brian noticed that Tertius was smiling, and he didn't like it.

"It's not that important," he said stiffly.

"May I come in?" asked a voice from the doorway. Brian glanced past Lianor, and his heart skipped a beat. It was Alys.

"Of course," said Lianor, picking up her basket. "I was just going."

"Let me help you, princess," said Tertius. He took the basket from her, and they went out together.

Alys came over to the bed. She was wearing a blue dress, the color of her eyes, with long, full sleeves. Her pale-gold hair was covered by a veil.

"My father told me that you were awake," she said. "I know that he thanked you for what you did yesterday. But I wanted to tell you how brave I thought you were."

"I wasn't brave," said Brian. "I was foolish."

"Foolish?"

"How could I have expected to overcome the Black Knight when he had already overthrown some of the greatest champions in England?"

"But still you challenged him. Why?"

"I think you know why, princess," he said with sudden boldness.

She flushed slightly, lowering her eyes. "Perhaps I do," she said. "How long will it take for your side to heal?"

"Just a few days. But your sister says it will be several weeks before I can use my arm again."

"I see. Of course there's no need for you to go immediately even then. Sir Uriel was not nearly so badly hurt when he fought the Black Knight at Yule, and he's still here."

"Oh? What's he like?"

"Sir Uriel? He's a most worthy knight and a very interesting man. He plays the harp beautifully, knows all about food and wine, and has been to the court at Camelot. He met the king and queen and can tell you everything about everyone there."

Brian felt a twinge of jealousy. "Has he fought in many tourneys?"

"Yes, I think so. Why?"

"I'd like to meet him."

"I'll tell him that. I must go now; there are things that I must do. But I'll stop in again."

"This afternoon?"

"Perhaps. If not then, tomorrow."

Smiling, she left. Shortly after that, one of the serving wenches brought him a bowl of soup. He finished it and fell asleep. When he woke, his headache was gone, and he found he had another visitor; a tall, rather limp man with straw-colored hair and long mustachios. He wore a bright scarlet tunic embroidered with gold thread and, standing just inside the open door, he looked very elegant and just a little vague.

"Hope I didn't wake you," he said. "Alys thought I should stop by; but when I got here, you were asleep."

"No, you didn't wake me," said Brian. "You must be Sir Uriel."

"What? Oh, yes. Thought you knew. Saw your joust with the Black Knight. Good show."

"Not good enough, unfortunately."

"Well, can't win 'em all, you know. Of course he's a swine—the Black Knight, I mean—demanding tribute and all that. But he's a rare jouster. Knocked me heels over crupper last Yule. Not too badly hurt, were you?"

"No. A broken collarbone and some ribs."

"Well, as long as it wasn't an arm or a leg. They're troublesome. Or your neck—that's even worse. You've a good seat, lots of dash. But you should learn how to fall."

"I suppose so. But I'd rather learn how *not* to fall."

"How not . . . ? Oh, very good. I'll have to remember that. Of course, if you had to get hurt, you couldn't find a better place to recover than this: comfortable quarters, good food. And, of course, the girls. Lianor's very nice, and besides being so practical, she's really quite pretty. And Alys . . . !"

"Yes," said Brian.

"You think so too, eh? Well, why not? It

was after I saw her that I decided to take a whack at the Black Knight. I usually stay away from that type, the ones who hove at fords and all; they're pretty rough customers as a rule. And I must say he set me down in short order. Of course I wasn't as badly hurt as you, but . . ." He had wandered over to the window while he was talking and now, looking down, his face brightened. "Afraid I have to go now. Hope you're up and about soon."

"Thank you," said Brian.

He lay there for a moment after Sir Uriel left. Then throwing back the sheet, he got out of bed. He caught his breath at the sudden stab of pain in his shoulder and side. When it had gone away, he went over to the window and looked out also. There was an enclosed garden just below the window. Climbing roses covered the walls, and there were hollyhocks and larkspur in the borders. There was a pool in the center of the close with water lilies in it, and Alys was strolling on the flagstone walk in the shade of an ancient linden.

Brian was still at the window when Tertius came in.

"I thought you were supposed to be wounded," he said. "Practically at death's door."

"You know I'm not," said Brian sullenly. "And anyway, there's nothing wrong with my legs. Where have you been?"

"To see my friend, the goldsmith."

"Oh. Well, I'm glad you have a friend here."

"You mean you don't think you have?"

"I don't know." Then, as Tertius studied him, "My head's starting to hurt again."

"It generally does when you've had a concussion. Why don't you get back into bed where you belong?"

"I think I will."

The next morning Brian felt not only better, but stronger. Again he got up, more carefully this time, and began to dress himself. It wasn't easy with only one hand, but he managed quite well until he tried to pull on his tunic. It caught on the elbow of his bad arm, and he was tugging at it, swearing under his breath, when he heard Lianor say, "Stop that!"

Coming into the room, she untied the sling, eased his arm through the armhole of the tunic, then tied the sling again.

"I don't remember telling you that you could get up," she said.

"You didn't tell me I couldn't."

"I thought you'd have sense enough to know you shouldn't. How do you feel?"

"All right."

"Then I think you can stay up. But stop prowling about like a pard in a cage. Sit down."

"Why?"

"Because if you don't, you'll give yourself another headache. And I don't think you'd like the potion I'd give you to cure it."

Moodily he went over to a bench near the window and sat down. He had already looked out into the garden. Alys wasn't there.

"She's in the solar," said Lianor. "With Sir Uriel."

"Who?" asked Brian.

"The Queen of Cappadocia," she said. "Who do you think?" And when he didn't answer, "You don't know what to do with yourself, do you?"

"No."

"Do you play chess?"

"Yes. Not very well."

Going to one of the chests, Lianor took out chessmen and a board, set the board on the bench, and they began to play. Brian's eyes kept straying from the board to the garden below, and they hadn't made a dozen moves before Lianor said, "Check."

He moved his king.

"That does it," said Lianor, bringing up a bishop. "Mate. Well, you were honest about that."

"About what?"

"The fact that you don't play very well."

"I was thinking about something else," said Brian.

"I know. Do you want to play another?"

"No."

"I don't blame you. I'd only beat you again."

Picking up the board and chessmen, she put them back in the chest. Then, nodding coolly to him, she left the room. He remained at the window for some time. Alys didn't walk in the garden that day, but she did stop in to see how he was late in the afternoon.

CHAPTER SEVEN

LIANOR SHRUGGED. "You can try it if you like," she said. She watched as he slipped his arm out of the sling, raised it and brought it forward across his chest. "This isn't the first time you've done that, is it?"

"How did you know?" asked Brian.

"Because of the way you moved it. You knew where it might hurt. When was the first time?"

"A few days ago. I got tired of dressing with only one hand."

"Very intelligent. It takes weeks for a bone to mend properly. And if it doesn't . . . How does it feel?"

"Fine. Wait, I'll show you."

Taking his sword from the peg on the wall, he buckled it on, drew it and cut right and left. He had tried this before also, but this time it barely hurt at all.

"Splendid," said Lianor dryly. "Would you like me to take your challenge to the Black Knight?"

"Don't bait me. I know it's not entirely well yet. But is there any reason why I can't ride now if I'm careful?"

"You're very anxious to leave here, aren't you?"

"Yes and no. I'll never forget all you've done for me. You've been very kind . . ."

"What about Alys?"

He flushed. "I asked you not to bait me. She's been kind too. Everyone has. But I was thinking about Tertius."

"Ah, yes. That quest of yours. Well, if you're so eager to go, I don't know why you can't."

"When?"

"Whenever you'd like."

"Thank you, princess."

Pulling off the sling, he hurried out of the room and down the stairs. During the weeks he had been there, he had gotten to know the castle almost as well as he knew Caercorbin. It had been a curious period in which time had seemed disjointed and oddly inconstant: now going quickly, now dragging tediously. Though Lianor, who was the castle chatelaine, had many more duties than her sister, somehow he had seen more of her than of Alys. It was Lianor who had taken him to the armory where the armorer was mending his hauberk and shown him the stillroom where she compounded her salves and distilled sweet essences out of herbs. He had gone hawking with her several times, watching her fly her merlin in the fields outside the town. But while Alys had less to do—and here was the rub—when he did see her, it was rarely alone. When she walked in the close or sat in the solar doing needlework, Sir Uriel or some other knight was almost always with her. And listening to them play or sing for her and hearing their pretty speeches and talk of other courts made Brian feel awkward and out of place, and he would soon leave.

There was always Tertius, of course. But though they saw each other every day and sat together when they dined in the great hall, there were times when he disappeared. For he went almost every day to the shop of his friend, the goldsmith. And since he never told Brian what he did there—and Brian was too proud to ask him—Brian in turn talked little to him, so there was a slight coolness between them.

Since it was midmorning, Brian found Alys in the close and, beyond expectation, found her alone. While Lianor seemed to like the hot summer sun, going bareheaded until she was golden brown, Alys, who was fair, avoided it and only sat or strolled in the walled garden early in the day or late in the afternoon.

She was sitting on a stone bench in the shade of the linden tree and smiled as he came toward her.

"Greetings, princess," he said. "May I sit with you awhile?"

"I wish you would. This embroidery is beginning to bore me. Besides, my tiring woman tells me that if I do needlework out-of-doors it will give me a squint and wrinkles."

"Nature could not be so unkind to us as to let anything mar your beauty."

"You're very gallant today. And you also seem more cheerful than you've been of late."

"Why should I not be when I've witnessed a miracle?"

"What miracle is that?"

"Finding you alone."

"Is that such a rare thing?"

"Rarer than strawberries at Yuletide, and much more welcome. But besides that, I've had good news. My shoulder, it seems, is well again."

"Of course. Your sling—I should have noticed. It is all well?"

"Well enough so that I can ride."

"You mean ride from here? Leave here?"

"Yes, princess."

"Then let me take back what I said about your gallantry. For I find it not at all gallant that you should be so happy to leave us."

"You know it's not that, princess—that I want to go. But we've been here for many weeks now. . . ."

"And you're anxious to be off on that mysterious quest of yours. Well, I can't keep you. Nor would I if I could. But when it's accomplished, perhaps you'll come back again."

"Would you like me to come back?"

She looked at him from under lowered lashes. "Need you ask that?"

"Then I promise that when I have done something worthy—and to be worthy of you it must be worthy indeed—I will come back."

"When will you go? Will it be soon?"

"I don't know. I must talk to Tertius about that. But . . ."

He noticed that she wasn't looking at him, but past him.

"Good morning, Sir Uriel," she said. "If it is still morning."

"Good morning, princess," he said. "Of course it's still morning. It's only . . . Oh. You mean it's late. Well, the fact is . . ."

"You needn't explain," she said. "And you needn't go, Brian."

"Of course not," said Sir Uriel. "How are you today? How's the shoulder?"

"Better, thank you, Sir Uriel. I'm afraid I must go, princess. Tertius doesn't know yet. That we can leave now, I mean."

"In that case . . ." Alys held out her hand to him and, as he bent over it, "it will take you some time to get ready, so I will see you again. In the meantime, remember your promise."

"It shall be as a lodestone to draw me back here again."

Brian was standing at the window when Tertius came into the room. Tertius glanced at him, at the sling that lay on one of the chests, and raised an inquiring eyebrow.

"Yes," said Brian. "Lianor said I needn't wear it anymore. We can go whenever you'd like now."

"Why whenever I'd like?"

"I thought you were getting impatient, anxious to go."

"I am. But what about you?"

"I've already told Alys we were going."

"You don't sound very happy about it."

"I suppose I'd be happier if the quest we were on weren't just yours. I mean, if I had one too, one of my own."

Tertius peered at him. Then, reaching into his purse, he took out a curious object: two circular pieces of glass like the one he wore around his neck, but joined together by a silver bridge and with a curved silver wire on the side of each glass. Raising it, he slipped the wires behind his ears and looked at Brian again through the bits of glass. "What's that?" asked Brian.

"A pair of spectacles. I said something to you about them the first time we met."

"Oh, yes. How they'd help you see better. Do they?"

"Yes."

"Where did you get them?"

"The goldsmith made them for me. I thought if he could cut and polish gems, he should be able to grind lenses."

"So that's what you were doing over there almost every day."

"What did you think I was doing?"

"I didn't know, but I didn't like it. Your not telling me, I mean."

"You never asked me. And besides, I had a feeling that there were things you weren't telling me."

"I don't know what you mean," said Brian awkwardly.

"Don't you? All right. But you were saying you'd be happier if you had a quest of your own. What sort of quest?"

"It wouldn't really matter if it was a good one. But perhaps something to do with Meliot." He gestured toward the window. "I keep looking out and thinking of what's happening here—of what the Black Knight has done to the town, the whole kingdom—and wishing there were something I could do about it, something to help."

"Why don't you find the Knight with the Red Shield?"

Brian stared at him.

"What?"

"I said why don't you find the Knight with the Red Shield? If what they say is true and only he can overthrow the Black Knight . . . Easy!" For Brian had clutched him in a bear hug. "You'll break my spectacles."

"No, I won't. Tertius, what would I do without you?"

"I sometimes wonder," said Tertius, taking off the spectacles. Then, as Brian seized his arm and began dragging him toward the door he muttered, "Now what?"

"It's noon. The king will still be in the solar. Come on."

It was the king's custom, when he had finished his audiences in the throne room, to retire to the solar where he could be private and spend some time with his seneschal, Sir Amory. On this day, Alys, Lianor and Sir Uriel were there too: Sir Uriel talking to Alys while Lianor sat nearby with her account book on her lap. The king looked up as Brian and Tertius came in.

"Well, Brian," he said. "My daughters have given me two kinds of news about you, good and bad. The good that you are whole and hale again, and the bad that you intend to leave us."

"Both are true, Your Majesty. Though I cannot believe that our leaving can be called bad news."

"When you have shown yourself to be such a good friend to Meliot? You are either too modest or you care too little for our gratitude."

"It is we who are your debtors, Your Majesty, for your great courtesy and hospitality and," bowing to Lianor, "for the care that I was given."

"Could we do less than care for you when you got hurt trying to help us? You must know that you would be welcome here for as long as you chose to stay. But since I have been told that you have affairs of your own in hand, we will not try to keep you."

"The quest was not mine. Your Majesty. It was that of my friend, Tertius. But now I have one of my own."

"And is it just as mysterious and secret as his?"

"No, Your Majesty. And since it concerns you and Meliot, I thought you should know of it. You spoke of my attempt to be of help. As you know, that came to naught. But Tertius here has suggested a way in which I might truly be of service. And that is to find the one man in the world who can free you from the Black Knight: the Knight with the Red Shield." Then, as the king glanced at Sir Amory, "Why do you smile, Your Majesty?"

"Forgive me, Brian," said the king. "That you should consider such an undertaking puts us more in your debt than ever. But I must tell you that this is something that we have tried ourselves. For some years now I have been sending out men to search for the Knight with the Red Shield, not only throughout Britain, but in all parts of the civilized world. And so far no one has been able to find him or even find anyone who ever heard of him."

"But he must exist. Did not Merlin say . . . ?"

"Yes. But if Merlin was human, as I assume he was, would he not have been as fallible as the rest of us?" Then, "Again I ask your pardon, Brian. Why should I, of all men, try to discourage you from a venture that would be our salvation? Though I find it difficult to let myself hope, it does not follow that because others have failed, you will also. And," glancing at Alys and Lianor, "know this. If you succeed, there is nothing in all Meliot you could not have for the asking."

As with Lianor earlier, Brian felt himself flushing; but he managed to say, "To have been of service, Sire, would be reward enough."

"There are some," said the king, smiling, "to whom that might sound less than gallant."

"I only meant . . ."

"I know, Brian. And if you accomplish what you hope, we shall talk of this again. Meanwhile, Sir Amory will wait on you and see that you are provided with anything you require."

"I thank Your Majesty," said Brian. He and Tertius bowed. As they straightened up, prepared to withdraw from the solar, Brian's eyes met those of Alys. They were wide and bright, shining as they had before his joust with the

Black Knight. He glanced at Lianor. Her face was expressionless, her eyes strangely dark.

Sir Uriel caught up with them in the corridor outside.

"I say, that was a smashing idea you had there. About the Knight with the Red Shield, I mean. Wish I'd thought of it."

"I didn't think of it either," said Brian. "It was Tertius who did."

"Oh?" He looked Tertius up and down as if he were seeing him for the first time. "You know what they say—out of the mouths of babes and all that. Been here for more than six months, and it never occurred to me."

"Possibly you had other things on your mind," said Tertius.

"Perhaps I did. But now, you don't mind if I take a whack at it too, do you? Looking for old Red Shield, I mean."

"Not at all," said Brian.

"Good. Hoped you wouldn't. Perhaps we could join forces. When are you leaving?"

"As soon as we can," said Brian. "Tomorrow morning."

"Very early," said Tertius.

"That's not so good. Things to take care of, good-byes and such. Besides I hate getting up early—never at my best then. So perhaps we'd better go our own ways, what?"

"Perhaps we'd better," said Tertius gravely.

"Right. Probably see you sometime before you leave. If I don't, good questing!"

CHAPTER EIGHT

BY THE LIGHT of the stableboy's horn lantern, Brian looked over the sumpter mule for the last time, making sure the girth was tight and the well-filled saddlebags secure. Gaillard, eager to be off, nuzzled him, and Brian stroked his sleek neck. Then, satisfied that all was in order, he nodded to Tertius and mounted. Leading the mule, and with Tertius following, he rode out of the yard.

It had been dark when they woke, not only because it was so early, but because of a mist that had drifted down the river valley and blanketed the town in damp, gray obscurity. They had spent most of the afternoon before with Sir Amory, going over the provisions they would need, and had retired early, saying their good-byes to the king, Alys and Lianor in the great hall. Later, remembering the look in Alys's eyes as he bent over her hand, Brian was sure he would not sleep that night. But he had gone off almost as soon as he had climbed into the great canopied bed and had only awakened when Tertius shook him.

They crossed the town square and went down the narrow street that led to the gate, the echoes of the horses' hoofs sounding hollow, muffled by the fog. It felt odd to be riding without a lance and Sir Amory had been surprised when Brian had refused one, saying he would not be jousting for some time. He had been just as surprised when Brian had asked for a bow and some well-fletched arrows, but he had agreed that they might prove useful if their provisions ran low.

The captain of the guard came out of the gatehouse as they approached and, recognizing them, saluted and called an order to his men.

The heavy gate swung open, and they rode through it, turning left toward the river. But they had gone only a short distance when Gaillard shied and started to rear.

Steadying him, Brian leaned forward, peering through the mist. An old crone stood in the road, almost under Gaillard's nose. She wore a ragged, shapeless cloak; her face was weather-beaten, dark as a gypsy's, her gray hair tangled in elf-locks and her eyes red-rimmed and bloodshot.

"A boon, Sir Knight," she said in a harsh, croaking voice. "I crave a boon!"

"I am not a knight," said Brian. "I am only a squire. But if it lies within my power to grant what you wish, I shall."

"Do you pledge me your word on that?"

"I have said so, madam. Knight or squire, I keep my promises."

"Then I would go with you on your quest."

"What? How do you know that we are on a quest?"

"I know many things that are hidden from

others," she said, grinning. "As you will discover."

"But . . ." Brian turned to Tertius who had ridden up beside him and was studying the old woman. "What shall we do?"

"In the first place, foolishly or not, you gave your word. And in the second place, it's not uncommon for a helper to appear at the beginning of a quest."

"A helper?"

"You'll find them all through folklore." Then, as Brian looked at the old crone again, "I should not have to tell you that all that is white is not milk nor all that is dark, evil."

"That may be so," said Brian. "But we're not going maying or on a pilgrimage where we can sleep soft in inns. Our way will be long and hard."

"It could well be longer and harder without her."

"I was not thinking of us, but of her."

"Her age? Old oak is tougher than green. I doubt that she'll prove a burden. If she does, we can always find some place to leave her."

Still Brian hesitated. Then, "Very well, madam," he said. "You may come with us."

Her eyes gleamed. "Since it's not my custom to thank any man for anything," she said, "I will not thank you. But you should thank your friend. For it would have gone ill with you if you had refused me."

Putting her fingers to her lips, she whistled shrilly and a great, rawboned, sulphur-yellow mare came cantering out of the murk. Seizing the reins, the crone swung up into the saddle more like a young girl than an old woman. "I am Brian of Caercorbin, madam. And this . . ."

"I know your names, your quest, everything about you," she said.

"But we know nothing about you. What shall we call you?"

"Maudite," she said.

"But doesn't that mean . . . ?" He looked at Tertius, who nodded.

"Yes. Accursed, wretched, ill-favored."

"I shall never call you that," said Brian firmly. "I shall call you Maude."

"My, but our skin is thin," she said mockingly. "Call me what you like."

She fell in beside him as he touched Gaillard with his heels, and they rode in silence till they reached the ford. The mist was even thicker there, lying in eddying coils on the river's face. It was so thick that they could not see the further bank, but over the soft rush and murmur of the water they could hear the clank of metal as the Black Knight's men-at-arms walked back and forth on patrol.

Tertius and Maude started forward, but Brian said, "Wait," and, as they looked at him, surprised, "we cannot cross here."

"You need not fear the Black Knight," said Maude. "He keeps to his eyrie and only flies at noble game. While his guards will question us and may charge us toll, they will not turn us back."

"That is why I will not cross here," said

Brian. "If I could win my way through by force of arms, I would. But I will not pay toll to anyone or ask any man's leave to go where I choose."

"Hoity-toity," said Maude. "Not just thin-skinned, but high and mighty, too. Then your quest is over before it's begun. For there is no other ford, no other way through the forest."

"But there is," said a voice behind them. They turned. There on the bank, shrouded in mist, stood a tall figure. Even if he had not been leaning on a bow, they would have known him.

"You remind me," said Brian, "of the great Boar of Arvon who could not be found when he was hunted, but only appeared when he was not expected."

"He lived longer that way," said Hugh, "and I hope to do so also." Then, looking curiously at Maude, "I see you have a new companion."

"Yes," said Brian. "What are you doing here?"

"Waiting for you. We went north to the shooting match after all."

"And won the silver arrow?"

"Of course. The men of the marches may use bows, but there's naught like the greenwood to sharpen your eye. We were on our way home when we heard about your joust with the Black Knight. And about your quest."

"But it was only yesterday that we decided on it."

"Which is why I waited. I knew you would not be long in starting. And I thought you might not like to use the Black Knight's ford or take his road through the forest."

"There are other ways, then?"

"One other. It is difficult and dangerous, in some ways more dangerous than facing the Black Knight himself, but . . ."

"Will you show it to us?"

Hugh glanced at him, the sky, then studied the ford. "I have never tried it by daylight. And never with horses. But with this mist for cover . . . yes, I'll show it to you. This way."

He led them upstream, keeping to the river's edge. The bank to their left became higher and steeper until they were moving in single file at the foot of a cliff. From walks on the cliff when his shoulder was mending, Brian knew that the cliffs on the other side were even higher and steeper, which was why the ford was the only crossing. Coming to a huge rock that jutted out into the river, Hugh halted.

"It will be a wet passage," he said.

"If you do not mind, we do not," said Brian.

"Since when did a forest man mind the wet?" said Hugh and, holding his bow above his head, he walked out into the stream, feeling his way carefully. Brian followed him, leading the pack mule, with Maude and Tertius coming behind. The water became deeper, up to Hugh's armpits and, when they were clear of the rock, the full force of the current hit them. But they pressed on across. Once the mule stumbled and would have been swept downstream had not Brian, wincing at the strain on his newly healed shoulder, held him by the reins. The mule regained his footing, and they went on. At last the river became shallower, and a few minutes later they were on a shelving bank under the cliffs on the far side.

Now Hugh turned right, going downstream to where a copse of willows and alders grew at the water's edge. He worked his way through them, going in toward the cliff and, when Brian and the others followed him, they found that the trees had masked a narrow cleft or fault in the cliff. Signaling them to dismount, Hugh took the mule's reins and went before them over the talus of loose stones and into the cleft. They followed, leading their horses. The cleft was so narrow that they had to go in single file. It would have been dark there even in full daylight, for small trees grew in crevices in the rock walls, shadowing the cleft; and in the mist they had to feel their way. Moisture dripped on them from above and, when Tertius's palfrey stumbled on the wet stones, Hugh frowned back at him. Then the bottom of the cleft began rising and, a short while later, they were on level ground in the midst of the forest.

Putting his finger to his lips, Hugh pointed to the right. There on a knoll—massive, sombre, and brooding—was a keep, and Brian knew that this must be the stronghold of the Black Knight. The stones in the lower courses of the walls were huge, cyclopean, and looked as if they had been worked into place—by what art he could not imagine—in time long past. The upper part of the walls, though covered with ivy, were newer; and it was clear that this was an ancient, ruined fortress, which the Black Knight had seized for his own and rebuilt until it was impregnable.

They were in the rear of the keep, for there was no sign of an entrance. But even there guards were on watch for, hearing the clink of mail, Brian looked up and saw a man-at-arms walking the battlement and scanning the forest below. He disappeared behind the tower and Hugh led them on, away from the keep and the road it guarded and deeper into the forest.

When they were well away, Hugh gestured to them to mount, gave the mule's reins to Brian and began to go more quickly, jogging ahead of them in a tireless woodsman's trot. The mist had begun to thin but, though it was midmorning, it was still dim. The great forest trees grew so thickly that the sunlight could not find its way through their leaves. Finally Hugh stopped.

"I will leave you now," he said. "The Black Knight's men do not come to this part of the forest so you are safe from them and him. As for the other danger I spoke of . . ."

"I know about that," said Maude, "and I will deal with it."

"You know?" said Hugh, looking at her sharply. "How do you know?" And when she did not answer, but only smiled a small, enigmatic smile, he shook his head. "If you knew that, then you must also have known of the hidden way here."

"Perhaps."

"Then why did you say that there was no other ford, no other way through the forest?"

She shrugged, still smiling secretly but saying nothing. Hugh continued to study her with growing distaste and uneasiness.

"For myself, I would not journey with you for a capful of bezants," he said. "Still, since the devil cares for his own, one might do worse than have you for a guide in these parts." Then, turning and starting back the way he had come, he murmured, "Fare you well, Brian."

"Wait, Hugh," called Brian. "I have not thanked you yet."

"The best thanks you can give him," said Maude, "is to let him go."

"Why?" asked Brian. "And what is this danger he talked of?"

"It would be better if you never knew," she said. "But since the moon is almost full, I do not think you will be so fortunate."

Urging her mare forward, she brushed past him and began leading the way. Brian exchanged looks with Tertius, then they rode after her.

All day they rode through the forest, sometimes through open glades, sometimes along narrow tracks. They stopped only once at a mossy spring to rest, water their horses and eat some bread and cheese. While they were eating, Brian looked up at the sun and said, "We are riding east."

"Which way would you go?" asked Maude.

"I don't know since I don't know where I will find what I am seeking."

"Then it does not matter whether we ride north, east, or south." Her hood was pulled forward, shadowing her face. "But when—or if—you do find what you are seeking, what then?"

"What do you mean?"

"You have been promised a reward if you find the Knight with the Red Shield and bring him back to Meliot. But if you do, and if he overthrows the Black Knight, will he not wish to be rewarded too? And will not his reward be the one you want for yourself, the fair white hand of the Princess Alys?"

For a moment Brian stared at her and, seeing

the shock in his eyes, she threw back her head and laughed shrilly.

"Stop that!" said Brian angrily.

"Forgive me, noble master," she said, bowing low. "I forgot about your thin skin. I should not have laughed. More important, I should not have told you something you did not want to hear, something you should have thought of yourself."

"I did not think of it for a reason you would not understand. Because I want no reward!"

"No? Then the more fool you!" Rising, she whistled to her mare and mounted as lightly as she had before. "Do we continue eastward?"

"You said it did not matter which way we went."

"Then we will go where Gracielle takes us." And, without waiting for them or looking back, she gave the mare her head and set off again.

"I begin to think that Hugh was right," said Brian, mounting also. "And now we know why she is called Maudite."

"Which you said you would never call her," said Tertius. "She asked to come with us, but she never pretended to have a honeyed tongue."

"So far it has been more like an adder's," muttered Brian. "Why did she want to come? What is her errand?"

"If she is a helper, it is to help us."

"And if she's not?"

"Ask her if you like. I doubt if she'll tell you, but in time perhaps we'll find out."

They rode on through the afternoon, past huge fallen trees and tangles of briars, circling marshy places and fording streams. It was a silent ride for they spoke but little and the rotting mold underfoot muffled the sound of the horses' hoofs.

As the sun sank in the west, they came to an open place near a reed-fringed pool. A stream ran through the glade into the pool and, when Maude turned and looked inquiringly at Brian and Tertius, they nodded. After they had unsaddled the horses and the mule, watered them and set them to grazing, Brian took his bow and went down to the pool. He found a flock of wild ducks feeding there and shot two before they flew off in alarm. Pleased with himself, he went back to the glade. But when Maude saw the ducks, she said, "I am not one of your queasy-stomached, finicky eaters, but I am not overly fond of raw meat."

"You're right," said Brian, disconcerted. "We have no fire." But remembering Tertius's burning glass, he asked, "Couldn't you . . . ?"

"No," said Tertius. "The sun is too low."

"I have fire," said Maude. "But this is not the time or the place for one."

"Why?" asked Brian.

"Because it's too dangerous," she said shortly. "Still, there are dangers in not having one, too. Perhaps we could risk it."

Going to one of her saddlebags, she took out a small earthenware pot and, when Brian and Tertius had gathered twigs and tinder, she shook out some embers and blew them into flame. They built a fire and roasted the ducks on spits of green wood. It was dark when they had finished eating, and Brian and Tertius wrapped themselves in their cloaks and stretched out on the fine grass of the glade. Maude, however, sat huddled on the far side of the fire, still and apparently listening to the forest sounds: the faint snap of a twig as a boar or other animal circled the clearing, the distant hoot of a hunting owl. As the fire died down, its faint glow worked a kindly magic on Maude. She had thrown back the hood that had shadowed her face during the day and, with the half-dark hiding her gray hair, wrinkles and bloodshot eyes, she did not seem as aged as she had, and it could also be seen that once she had been more than comely.

Looking at her, Brian marveled that after their long ride that day, one of her years should seem no more weary than he was himself. And he wondered again at her mission, why she had asked to come with them, and also what the danger was that both she and Hugh had talked of. And wondering, he fell asleep.

A scream woke him. He opened his eyes, not sure that he hadn't dreamed or imagined it until he saw Maude standing tensely by the embers of the fire. It came again, thin and high and so distant that he could not tell whether it was human or not. That time it was followed by the far-off breaking of branches as something crashed through the underbrush. Then came shrieks, ululating cries and a howling as if a pack of frenzied hounds were hot on the trail of their quarry.

Brian was on his feet, as was Tertius.

"Quickly!" said Maude, trampling on what remained of the fire. "Help me with this!"

They joined her in stamping out the last of the coals and remained close together in the darkness.

"What is it? " whispered Brian. "What . . . ?"

She silenced him as the crashing in the underbrush drew nearer. The scream sounded again, not more than a hundred yards from the clearing, and Brian sensed rather than saw that Maude had moved away and was standing between them and whatever it was that ranged the forest. Then, panting, screeching, howling, the eerie and invisible hunters swept by in close pursuit. They stood where they were until the last faint cry died away in the distance.

"Go back to sleep," said Maude. "The danger is past. For tonight at least."

Brian took his hand from his sword.

"But what . . . ?" he began.

"I said go to sleep!" said Maude.

Meekly, Brian and Tertius returned to their places, wrapped themselves in their cloaks and stretched out again. Sometime later Brian stirred and opened his eyes. The moon, almost full, had risen, and by its pale light he saw that Maude was where she had been before, huddled on the far side of the trampled embers, keeping a lonely vigil. At this, the last of the anger he had felt toward her left him and, reassured, he closed his eyes again and slept soundly.

CHAPTER NINE

WHEN BRIAN WOKE the next morning, Maude was already up, raking over the ashes of the fire for embers, which she put in her earthenware pot with twigs, moss and tinder to keep them smoldering. She said nothing about what had happened the night before and neither did Brian nor Tertius. They ate some bread to break their fast and then set off, riding east through the forest. That night again, just before the moon rose, they heard the screeching and the howls as the spectral hunt went by near them in the darkness; and they heard it yet again the night following.

Late on the afternoon of the next day, the third of their journey, the forest became less dense, the undergrowth thinner, and the soil drier and more sandy. Once more they camped by a small stream, built a fire and ate some of the provisions they had brought with them. When darkness closed in and Brian and Tertius wrapped themselves in their cloaks, Maude sat as before on the far side of the fire. But on this night it seemed to Brian that she was more restless than uneasy. Several times she rose and went to the edge of the trees as if listening for something. Watching her and wondering about the many things he had wondered about before, he fell asleep.

This time it was not the wild sounds of the hunt, but music that woke him: music so faint and distant that, as with the scream on their first night in the forest, he was not sure that he had truly heard it. He sat up. The moon, full now, was just rising above the treetops, and by its pale light he saw Maude standing near the edge of the clearing, listening. Then it came again: a thin, clear piping, a tinkling as of cymbals and a soft, sweet chanting.

Glancing at Tertius, Brian saw that he was awake and listening also. They both rose, went toward Maude. But by the time they reached the place where she had been standing, she was gone, walking in the direction from which the music was coming. They hurried after her, and when she heard their footsteps, she paused, waiting for them.

"Where are you going?" asked Brian.

"Out there." She hesitated a moment, studying them. "If you like, you can come too."

They went on together, along an aisle of trees whose branches met high overhead like the vault of a cathedral. The music swelled, reached a climax, and died away, but Maude continued on and they with her. Then, abruptly, the trees ended. They were on the edge of a heath and there, some hundred yards away, were the Standing Stones.

They were awesome in the clear, cool light of the moon: a half-dozen huge gray stones set upright in a crescent with one slab lying flat before them like a table. More slowly now they walked toward them and, as they drew near, Brian saw that someone stood within the half circle of stones, behind the flat slab.

She was tall: even with the huge stones behind her that should have dwarfed her, she seemed taller than a man. And she was beautiful with the cold, flawless beauty of moonlight on snow. She wore a flowing robe that was sheer and shimmering as gossamer. Gems gleamed in her hair, seeming to twinkle like distant stars as she moved.

"You may approach," she said in a voice that was low but clear as a silver bell. She watched them with great, gray eyes as they came toward her. When they were before her, Maude dropped to her knees and Brian and Tertius did her a deep reverence.

"Rise, child," she said to Maude, and there was nothing odd in her speaking thus to someone so old. Then, when Maude was standing again, "You of course I know, as you know me. You," to Tertius, "I think I know. Do you know me?"

"Yes, my lady," said Tertius. "At least, I know who you are."

"Oh? Name no names—I have too many. But if you know, give me a sign."

Drawing his dagger, Tertius scratched a triangle in the bare, hard-packed earth, the point of the triangle downward.

"Another," she said.

Next to the triangle he drew a circle set on top of a tau cross.

"Now a third."

He drew three long-necked birds flying, either herons or cranes.

"Yes," she said. "Now I remember who you are. The third reminded me. That Merlin!" She smiled. "What about you?" she said to Brian. "Do you know me or aught about me?"

"No, my lady. Only what my eyes tell me."

"And what do they tell you? No, you need not answer. That will do well enough. That and the company in which you come. Now what is it you wish?"

"Nothing, my lady," murmured Maude, and her voice was not harsh and hoarse as it usually was, but soft and musical.

"Nothing? Then why did you come here to this place at this time?"

"To pay you homage."

"I see. That's very gratifying. But do you not have questions you would like to have answered?"

"One always has questions, my lady."

"Naturally. Well, let us see what we can do."

She waved her hand and a cloud drifted across the moon's face and in the dimness a strange transformation took place. The Standing Stones seemed to change into a half-circle of tall black boxes with spinning spools on their faces and winking, blinking lights; the boxes all humming and buzzing as if they were alive. The flat slab became smooth and on it there was a row of smaller boxes, also with blinking lights, and many curious knobs and buttons. "Is that a 501, my lady?" asked Tertius politely.

"Why would I want anything that big?" she said testily. "But since I can't possibly keep everything I'm supposed to know in my head, I have started using their information storage and retrieval system." She looked at Maude. "You first, my dear. What is it you wish to know?"

Maude returned her glance for a moment, then lowered her eyes.

"Oh," said the White Lady. "Of course." She pushed a button, turned a knob and a bell rang. "The answer is yes. Now you," she said to Tertius.

"Will I find what I am seeking?" he asked.

Again she pushed the button, turned the knob, and again the bell rang.

"Same answer," she said. "Yes. Your turn," she said to Brian.

"I may ask any question I like?"

"Anything within reason. I don't like ones dealing with immortality or squaring the circle."

"Then where shall I find the Knight with the Red Shield?"

This time when she pushed the button and turned the knob, the bell rang many times and continued ringing until she pushed another button.

"Erratum. Unprogrammed for," she said severely. "You've asked the wrong question."

"I'm sorry. What's the right one?"

"The rule has always been only one to each. But since this is all new to you . . ." She turned a different knob, pushed the button. There was a rapid, clicking noise and a sheet of paper with some small but clear writing on it slid out of one of the boxes in front of her.

"The right question," she said, picking it up, "seems to be: How will I know the Knight with the Red Shield?"

"Very well," said Brian. "How will I know him?"

Again the White Lady pushed the button. Again there was a rapid clicking noise and another sheet of paper with the strange, small writing on it slid out on the flat surface in front of her. She picked it up, frowned and snapped her fingers. The cloud overhead parted and a shaft of moonlight shone down, illuminating the paper.

"You will know him by his sword," she read. "For it was forged of steel that is not of this earth. You will know him by his look. For he will have drunk from the dragon's horn and have known pity as well as fear. You will know him by his strength. For he will first have lost it and then regained it. And finally, you will know him because he does not know himself. And, accepting himself, he shall find that which he did not seek nor ever hoped to find."

She put down the paper. "Is that clear?" she asked.

"No, my lady," said Brian.

"Good," she said. "It's not meant to be. I'd give you a copy, but I don't think you'll need it. After all, there are three of you, and among you you should be able to remember it."

"But . . ." began Brian.

"I told you the rule was one question," she said. "And your answer was longer and more detailed than most."

"We thank you, my lady," said Maude, dipping low in a curtsy.

"You're welcome, my dear. Stop by any time when the moon is full." She paused, looking at each of them in turn. "As you said when you two met, Tertius, it should be a most interesting quest."

She waved her hand again and an even darker cloud drifted by above them, hiding not only the moon but the stars as well. When it had passed and the moon shone again, the Standing Stones were as they had been before and she was gone.

Brian glanced at Tertius, then at Maude. But Tertius avoided his eyes and Maude's hood was pulled forward so he could not see her face. It was she who moved first. Turning, she started back across the heath toward the camp, and they followed.

CHAPTER TEN

THEY SLEPT LATER than usual the next morning and when they finally broke camp, the sun was well up, almost as high as the treetops. They rode along the same aisle of trees that they had walked the night before and out onto the heath. To their left were the Standing Stones, looking smaller and less awesome than they had by moonlight.

Feeling the turf underfoot and seeing the wide, open spaces ahead of him, Gaillard tossed his head and strained at his bit. Brian turned the pack mule over to Tertius and, when he gave the great stallion his head, he went into a thundering gallop, stretching his muscles. They galloped for some time, finally pausing on the top of a rise. Behind them, running north and south, was the dark green of the forest. Ahead of them, as far as the eye could see, lay the heath. It was somewhat rolling, dotted with low, rounded hills and an occasional small lake. The only trees were thorn trees, stunted and wind-warped, and the only other things that grew there besides the rank grass were heather and fern. It was lonely, barren, empty country for nowhere was there a sign of human habitation.

All that day they rode across the heath, camping at night near one of the small lakes whose water was dark and tasted of peat. There was a rabbit warren nearby and, while Maude and Tertius built a fire, Brian went over to it with his bow and shot two rabbits. On his way back he stirred up a heath cock and, loosing at it without thinking, he dropped it as neatly as Long Hugh might have done. So that night they dined well.

The next day they rode on across the heath. But though it remained as empty and desolate as ever, about midmorning a strange feeling came over Brian: a feeling that they were being watched. As he checked Gaillard, he noticed that Maude had reined in her mare and was looking about also.

"Anything wrong?" asked Tertius.

"I'm not sure," said Brian. He glanced at Maude, and she nodded.

"There's someone about," she said.

"What makes you think so?" asked Tertius.

She shrugged, still looking around her, then pointed.

"That hill to the left. In the gorse near the top."

The hill was some distance away, four or five hundred yards. Shading his eyes, Brian studied it. And as he wondered how Maude could see so far with her old, bloodshot eyes, he saw a slight movement in the gorse.

"She's right," he said. "I'll go look."

"Wait," said Tertius.

Reaching into his saddlebag, he took out a

brass tube. It had a bit of polished glass at each end of it, like the glass of his spectacles. And it was apparently made of two sleeves, one fitting inside the other, for he pulled it out to twice the length it had first seemed to be.

"What's that?" asked Brian.

"A spyglass or telescope," said Tertius, raising it to his eye. "I had the goldsmith make it when he made my spectacles." He peered through it. "It looks like one of the Old People."

"The Old People?"

"They were here before the Saxons, before the Romans. Perhaps before the Beaker People. Here." He handed Brian the brass tube.

Brian looked through it as Tertius had done and stiffened, for the hill seemed to leap toward him until it was only a few yards away. Steadying the glass, he directed it at the top of the hill and caught a glimpse of a thin, dark face framed by gorse; the black eyes looking directly into his own. Then it disappeared.

"A useful thing," he said, handing the

telescope back to Tertius. "He's gone now, but I saw him. Friendly or unfriendly?"

"He didn't look very friendly to me," said Tertius. "But he may just have been curious. We'll see." Then, noticing that Maude was looking curiously at the spyglass, "Would you like to try it?" he asked, holding it out to her.

She took it tentatively, peered through it, and—like Brian—stiffened in surprise.

"You say you got it from a goldsmith?" she said, giving it back to him.

"I said I had him make it."

"Are you an enchanter?"

"Far from it."

"And you knew the White Lady's signs. You're a strange young man."

"No stranger a young man than you are an old woman."

"What do you mean?"

Tertius did not answer, merely looked at her, and it was Maude who dropped her eyes.

They rode on. Late that afternoon they came to a narrow place between two hills, both overgrown with bracken and heather. As Brian led the way through it, Gaillard snorted and shied. Brian leaned forward to quiet him, and a spear whistled from the underbrush, passing just over his head. With an exclamation, Brian drew his sword and sent Gaillard crashing through the heather in the direction from which the spear had come. But though he beat the bushes halfway up the hill, he found no sign of the hidden attacker.

When he returned to Maude and Tertius, they handed him the spear. The head was of flint, lashed to the shaft with sinew, but it was polished and sharp, a wicked weapon. They exchanged glances. Then, taking the spear in both hands, Brian broke the shaft over his saddlebow and tossed the two halves into the brush.

They rode more warily after that, avoiding narrow places and thick cover, keeping to the open. And that night, camping in a rocky valley, they kept a fire burning and took turns standing watch.

The next morning they made an early start, and by that afternoon, though the country through which they rode remained as desolate as ever, it became flatter and they caught glimpses of green to the south. They turned that way and, coming to marshes that bordered a sluggish river, went east again, riding parallel to the river.

As the sun slanted down and their shadows became long, they began looking about for a place to camp.

"What about that hill?" asked Brian, pointing to a grass-covered hillock of strangely regular shape.

"I don't think it's a hill," said Tertius. "I think it's a howe or grave mound."

"Whatever it is, it will shelter us from the wind," said Brian.

They unsaddled on its lee side, facing the

marshes; and after caring for their horses, they built a fire and had their supper. Since they had seen no enemy signs during the day, they set no watch; but Brian sat late over the dying fire, listening to the sough of the wind through the river reeds. It was an overcast, starless night, and finally his eyes grew tired of staring into the darkness and he slept.

A shrill sound woke him. It was much like the scream that they had heard in the forest, but this time it was nearer at hand, only a short distance away. Brian leaped to his feet, reaching for his sword—and it was not there!

As he fumbled with the empty sheath, bewildered and uncomprehending, the sound came again, and then he realized it was Gaillard neighing. Running to where the horse was tethered, Brian saw the great white stallion rearing and shaking his head, while a strange, slim figure clung to his halter. Hearing Brian's footsteps, the stranger dropped the halter and turned to flee, but Brian seized him, wrestling him to the turf. Though smaller than Brian, he was wiry and strong, and it was several minutes before Brian could pin him down.

Maude and Tertius were awake now also, calling to him.

"I'm over here," he shouted. "Bring a light."

Maude and Tertius came hurrying to him with a brand from the fire, and all three looked down at a man whose face was the twin of the one they had seen watching them from the gorse: thin and dark and with streaks of blue paint on his cheeks and forehead. His black hair was long and unkempt, and he wore a sleeveless sheepskin tunic. A stone axe hung from his belt, but there were bronze bracelets on his bare arms; these and the way he glared up at them despite his fear seemed to indicate that he was someone of consequence among his people.

"Some rope," said Brian, pulling him to his feet.

Tertius cut a length of rope from his horse's halter.

"The mule is gone!" he exclaimed. "And the saddlebags with our provisions!"

"That's not all that's gone," said Brian grimly. "They took my sword, too."

He tied the dark man's hands together and led him back to the fire, setting him against a rock.

"Who are you?" he asked. "What's your name?"

The dark man bared his teeth at him in a wolfish grin that was a mixture of fright and fierceness, but he did not answer.

"He doesn't understand," said Tertius.

Maude had been putting wood on the fire, building it up to a roaring blaze. Now she came over and stood looking down at the prisoner.

"I think he does," she said. Drawing a small dagger from somewhere inside her ragged garments, she kneeled and pressed its point against his throat. "At least, he understands this, don't you, my poisonous pet?"

The small, dark man tried to draw back, but

she advanced the dagger, keeping it pressed against his throat.

"Yes," she said. "He understands. Now what's your name?"

"Migbeg," he whispered.

"Very good," she said. "A fine Pictish name. Now tell us how many men you have out there?" She pointed to the darkness and held up her left hand. "Five? Ten?"

Staring at her in terrified fascination as a cornered rabbit might stare at a stoat, he raised his hands, dropped them, and raised them again.

"Twenty!" said Brian in dismay. "I could hold them off, even at night, if I were properly armed. But with my sword gone . . ."

"I don't think we need fear an attack, at least tonight," said Maude, still holding the prisoner with her eye. "After all, we have a hostage. Perhaps you'd better tell them that, Migbeg. Tell them," she jerked her head toward the surrounding darkness, "that if they attack," she gestured, "you die!"

Again Migbeg tried to draw back from the point of her dagger, but could not because of the rock behind him.

"You wouldn't really kill him, would you, Maude?" asked Tertius.

"You think not? What do you say, Migbeg?"

They read the answer in his face.

"See?" said Maude. "He knows. Very well, then, my pretty poppet. Tell them!"

For a moment Migbeg stared at her. Then, pushing the dagger to one side with his bound hands, he uttered a quavering call. Immediately there were answering calls from the darkness beyond the fire. Raising his voice, he spoke rapidly for a moment in a rasping, guttural tongue, ending on a rising, questioning note. There was a single, answering response from the darkness, and he nodded to Maude.

"Good," she said. "Now the two of you can sleep in peace."

"Why we?" asked Brian.

"Because I shall be keeping watch on our friend here."

"You shall not," said Brian. "If you like, you can keep the first watch. But you must promise to wake us and let us watch in turn."

"It is me he fears," said Maude, "far more than either of you. But if you insist . . . Very well."

And so they took turns keeping watch, as they had their second night on the heath. The next morning they broke their fast on some bread that had been part of their supper the night before. Maude protested when Brian gave some to Migbeg, pointing out that it was all the food they had.

"We can't let him starve," said Brian.

"He won't starve, missing a few meals," said Maude. "He'll just get hungry. But then so shall we, now that the mule and our provisions are gone."

"It's a grievous loss," said Brian. "But since I still have my bow and, with luck, should get us some rabbits or other game, I do not mind it as much as something else."

"Your sword?" said Tertius.

"Yes," said Brian. "Hostage or not, I won't feel easy till I'm armed again." He had been looking up at the hillock behind them as he spoke. "You said this was a grave mound. Who would be buried here?"

"A king or great chieftain of some sort," said Tertius. "I don't think it's one of the Old People's barrows. Possibly a Saxon, but probably a Norseman."

"Would he have been buried with his weapons?"

"Yes," said Tertius. "As a matter of fact, several famous swords have been found in howes like this. Of course, this one may already have been opened and robbed."

"Suppose we see. How does one get in?"

"Sometimes there's an entrance and sometimes there's not." He too had been studying the mound. Now he pointed to a flat rock some fifteen or twenty feet above them. "Let's try that."

Grass grew around the rock and at first it seemed too large and heavy for even two of them to move. But, working a thick branch under the edge of it, they were able to lever it up a few inches.

"Yes," said Tertius, peering under it. "There's a hole here. This may be the entrance."

Propping up the raised edge with stones, they were finally able to slide the rock to one side, exposing a square opening that slanted down sharply. It was some four feet high and Brian bent down to crawl into it.

"Wait!" said Maude from below them. "Don't go in there!"

"Why not?" asked Brian.

"Because he wants you to," she said, nodding toward Migbeg. "I saw it in his face as soon as you lifted the rock. There's some danger in there. Something . . . What is it?" she demanded fiercely. "Tell me!"

But though she threatened him with her

dagger, he only shook his head as if he did not know or did not have the words to answer her.

Tertius had been thinking, looking at Migbeg and then into the dark opening.

"Wait here," he said to Brian.

Going down to the fire, he brought back a brand.

"Here," he said, giving it to Brian. "Hold this in front of you and below your face."

Bending down, Brian crawled into the hole. By the light of the torch he could see that the tunnel had been made by men, for it was roofed with slabs of stone. It was awkward going, bent over under the low ceiling but, when he was some ten or twelve paces down the passage, he saw another opening ahead of him. He also saw something else: some white bones lying just inside the second opening. He thrust the torch down to see them better—and it went out!

"Tertius!" he gasped.

"Come back!" said Tertius. "Quickly!"

Brian needed no urging. His heart pounding, he crawled back out.

"Who . . . or what was it?" he asked, his voice unsteady.

"What, not who," said Tertius. "Some gas, probably methane or marsh gas." Brian looked at him. "An invisible vapor or exhalation that comes from decaying organic matter. It's sometimes found in mines where it's called firedamp."

"But how could it put out the torch?"

"Because a flame needs oxygen—air—to burn. As a matter of fact, under certain circumstances, methane itself will burn or explode. It has no odor and, if you had breathed enough of it, you would have died."

"Oh. I saw bones at the end of the passage."

"That was probably why Migbeg wanted you to go in. At some time, one or more of his people must have gone in and never come out again."

"And there's nothing we can do? No way . . ."

"If we leave the entrance open, the air will probably clear. But I don't know how long it will take." Again he thought for a moment. "There's something else we can try. Help me bring wood up here."

While Maude and Migbeg watched, Brian and Tertius gathered wood and built a fire at the entrance to the howe.

"What will this do?" asked Brian.

"Set up a convection current. The hot air, rising, will draw out the air from inside. At least, I hope it will."

Though some of the words Tertius used were strange to him, Brian remembered how the great fireplace at Caercorbin drew in smoke from all parts of the hall, and he thought he understood. They kept the fire burning for some time.

"Try it again," said Tertius at last. "The same way you did before, with the torch in front of you."

Once more Brian crawled into the opening.

Though the passageway was still damp, the air did not seem as heavy and oppressive as it had before. And this time the torch did not go out. He reached the bones he had seen before: the skeleton of a small man about the same size as Migbeg. Beyond, inside the second opening, lay another skeleton. Moving carefully so as to avoid them, Brian crawled through the second opening.

The roof above him was higher there and he stood up. He was in a square chamber, some dozen paces across and, sitting in a thronelike chair in the far corner and watching him with dark, baleful eyes was a still but menacing figure.

For a moment Brian stood frozen, his blood running chill. Then, raising the torch, he saw that this was a skeleton too, but that of a big man clad in a ring byrny and with a strange, horned helmet on his head. What Brian had thought were his eyes were the empty sockets of his skull.

Coins, chains and goblets of gold and silver lay in a heap before the seated figure, but Brian scarcely looked at this treasure. For lying across the dead man's knees was a sword.

Slowly he went forward.

"Sir," he said, "I know not your name or quality and ask your pardon for breaking in thus upon your rest. But my need is great. Naught else of yours, no part of your gold or silver will I touch. But, because of my great need, I ask leave to take your sword, giving you my word that I will never dishonor it."

He waited a moment, almost as if he expected a reply. Then, carefully, so as not to disturb those ancient bones, he drew the sword from its sheath.

In the distance, strangely muffled, he could hear Tertius calling anxiously to him.

"Coming," he called in answer.

Stepping back, he raised the sword in salute to the long dead warrior, then slipped it into his own sheath. His torch was beginning to smolder and burn more dimly, but he backed across the chamber as he would have from a royal presence or that of some great captain and only turned when he reached the low entrance.

Tertius's face cleared when he saw him.

"I was about to come in after you," he said. Then, his eyes went to the sword. "You found one."

"Yes," said Brian. "As you said, it was the tomb of some long dead chieftain; a Norseman by his arms and helmet. There was treasure there too. I took none of it, but," he glanced down at Migbeg, "there are others who might not hold their hands. So I think we should close it up again, leave it as we found it."

"I agree," said Tertius.

Together they levered the stone back over the entrance to the tomb, then went down to the camp.

Migbeg, with Maude guarding him, still sat against the rock, and both of them looked at Brian. As always, since Maude's hood was pulled forward, it was hard to see the expression on her face, but that on Migbeg's was a mixture of surprise and dismay.

"Well?" said Maude.

Brian drew the sword from his sheath. It was the first chance he had had to examine it, and he did so now with great interest. The hilt was of sea-ivory, checked and carved in ridges to ensure a secure grip, the pommel a great knob of amber. The blade was dark with oil or grease but, when Brian wiped it with a handful of dried grass, it remained blue-black, darker than any steel he had ever seen.

Tertius had put on his spectacles and in addition had taken out the glass he wore around his neck.

"May I see it?" he asked.

Brian gave it to him and together they bent over the blade. Despite the centuries it had lain in the howe, it was unmarred, with no sign of rusting or pitting, and both its edges were still incredibly keen. Down the center of the blade ran an inscription in strange, runic writing.

"Can you read it?" Brian asked Tertius.

"No," said Tertius. "But it comes from the

North and the steel is probably meteoric."

"Meteoric?"

"Meteors have often been found in the North. They're greatly prized because their iron has a high nickel content and makes a magnificent steel. You've done well," he said, giving the sword back to Brian. "It's a noble blade."

Taking it, Brian stroked the hilt, then gripped it. It fit his hand as if it had been made for him by some master swordsmith. It not only fit, but felt as familiar as if it was, in fact, his own sword that had been waiting there in the howe for centuries for him to come and claim it again. Though a shade heavier than the sword Sir Guy had given him, it was slightly shorter and its balance was such that he felt he could wield it for hours and not tire.

"I've done better than well," he said, raising it high and admiring its dark gleam. "It's an even finer sword than my old one. I shall call it Starflame."

CHAPTER ELEVEN

IT WAS NOW close to noon. Migbeg watched them as they saddled up and, noting his look, Brian said, "What shall we do with him?"

"He shall come with us," said Maude. "You have a sword now, but that does not mean we still do not need a hostage."

Brian turned to Tertius and he nodded. "It might be better," he said.

"Very well," said Brian. "He can ride with me."

"That would be very sensible," said Maude ironically, "to have him riding with you if you should have to use your precious sword."

"What then?"

"I will take him. Gracielle can carry double as well as Gaillard. But first . . ." She knelt before Migbeg, fixing him with her red-rimmed eyes. "Houses," she said, sketching one with her hands. "Which way?" She pointed in several directions, looking at him enquiringly. Raising his bound hands, Migbeg pointed southeast.

"Very good," she said. "How far?" She pointed to the horses, then to the sun. "One day's journey?" She held up one finger. "Two?"

Migbeg held up one finger.

"Ah," she said. "See what love and kindness can do? There are times when he seems almost human."

Remembering how she had overawed Migbeg with her dagger the night before, Brian smiled. She was a strange creature, he decided. But having become accustomed to her sharp tongue, he was not sorry that she was with them.

Lifting Migbeg to the saddle in front of Maude, Brian and Tertius mounted also, and they set off southeast. They rode that way all afternoon, following the river, which remained sluggish and fringed with marshes. The feeling that they were being watched remained strong; and when they came to a range of low hills, they began to catch glimpses of those who watched them: furtive figures who could be seen for a moment against the skyline, but who disappeared as they drew near.

When the first of these figures appeared, Brian loosened Starflame in its scabbard, but Maude said, "They will not attack." And Brian saw that she rode with her dagger ready in her hand, close to Migbeg's side.

Just before dusk, when they were thinking they would have to spend still another night on the heath, they saw a thin column of smoke ahead of them. Taking the spyglass from his saddlebag, Tertius peered through it and said, "He did not mislead us. It's a farmstead."

They rode on and soon came within sight of it: a goodly farm and byre surrounded by fields and pastures and with water meadows that ran down to the marshes that lay to the south.

They reined in their horses and, looking at Migbeg, Brian said, "Though he may have begun by doing ill, in the end he did well by us. I think we should let him go now. Agreed?"

"He did not help us by choice," said Maude. "I think he would have liked nothing better than to cut our throats. Still, unless we cut his, I do not know what else we can do with him, so . . . yes, I agree."

When Tertius nodded too, Brian dismounted and lifted Migbeg from Maude's horse. His dark eyes widened as Brian drew his dagger, but he stood there proudly and stoically. Then, as Brian cut the rope that bound his wrists and pointed to the heath, he stared in amazement.

Smiling at him, Brian handed him the stone axe that had hung from his saddlebow and pointed again toward the heath. Migbeg took his axe and stood there a moment longer looking at him. Then he turned and, though it was clear his impulse was to run, he walked off slowly. But he had not gone a dozen paces before he stopped and faced them once more. He studied them each in turn. Then, apparently making up his mind, he threw back his head and gave the quavering call he had given the night before. Immediately there was an answering call from a nearby rise. Brian stiffened, wondering whether it had been a mistake to release him after all, and again reached for Starflame. Raising his voice, Migbeg addressed the unseen watchers in his strange guttural tongue. There was silence, then a single voice with a note of protest in it, answered. Frowning, Migbeg spoke again, angrily and with authority. Again there was silence. Then a row of figures appeared on the crest of a hill some two hundred yards away. Some were dressed, like Migbeg, in sheepskin tunics, some wore short leather kilts, and one held the pack mule by his halter.

This last one came down the hill toward

them, leading the mule, and gave the halter to Migbeg. Walking back to them, Migbeg in turn gave the halter to Brian. Not only were the saddlebags with their provisions still on the mule but, thrust into one of them, was Brian's sword. Brian drew it out. Though Sir Guy had given it to him and at first he had felt lost without it, now it did not seem as much his own sword as Starflame. He glanced at Tertius. But, reading his thought, Tertius shook his head.

"I am not yet an armiger," he said. "It would be of no use to me."

"In that case," said Brian, "here." And reversing the sword, he held it out to Migbeg. Again Migbeg stared at him uncomprehendingly.

"Yes," said Brian. "I give it to you. Take it."

Slowly Migbeg reached for the sword. He examined it, feeling its keen edge. Then, his face alight, he thrust it through his belt. Stepping forward, he put his left hand on Brian's shoulder and with his right gripped his wrist. Brian did the same and for a moment they stood, looking into one another's eyes. Then Migbeg stepped back, saluted Brian—and after him Maude and Tertius—and went trotting off, followed by the man who had brought the mule.

"Well," said Maude. "I do not know what good it will do you, but you have made a friend."

"That's not why I did it," said Brian. "Though he came as a thief and would have killed us if he could, he was a brave man."

They waited until Migbeg reached the top of the ridge where his men surrounded him, patting and embracing him. Finally breaking free of them, he waved to the three below. They waved back and went on again.

When they reached the stead, the farmer stood outside the house, waiting for them. By his dress and bearing, he was a franklin or yeoman: a big, sturdy man with a brown beard and a pleasant, open face. His young wife stood by him and, holding her hand, was a golden-haired, blue-eyed girl of about six.

"Greetings," said the farmer. "I am Diccon of the Holm. Who are you and whence do you come?"

Brian gave their names, saying, "We were last of Meliot."

"Though that is far distant, I have heard of it," said Diccon. "But how did you come here? Not across the heath?"

"Yes."

"And had you no trouble with the Old Ones?"

"We had some," said Brian. "But it ended well."

"Then you are braver and more knowing travelers—or perhaps luckier—than most. For there are few who dare come that way."

"You have had trouble with them too, then?"

"No. My father's father worked out a peace with them, and they have observed it ever since. I would hear of your dealings with them, but there will be time for that. For you will eat and stay the night with us, will you not?"

Glancing at the others, Brian thanked him and said that they would, and they followed him into the house. A fire burned in the hearth, and a wonderful smell came from the huge iron pot that hung from a crane over the coals. They sat them down on benches and Diccon listened with great interest while Brian told them of their adventures on the heath. He nodded when Brian mentioned Migbeg's name, telling him that he was—as they had thought—an important chieftain and saying he was glad that things had turned out as they had. For, as he had mentioned before, his family had been at peace with the Old Ones, giving them food when they needed it during hard winters and sometimes trading with them for furs and skins.

During this time, while Diccon's wife was busy with the pot, the child had been observing them with grave, candid eyes. Now she came, not to Brian or Tertius, but to Maude and said, "What's your name?"

"Maude."

"I'm Amy. May I sit with you?"

Maude looked at her for a moment, startled. Then, "If you like," she said.

Despite the harshness of Maude's voice and her apparent indifference, Amy sat next to her on the bench and remained with her all through supper.

The stew that Diccon's wife, Nan, served them was as good as it had smelled, a welcome change from the game and salt meat they had been eating since they left Meliot. Afterward Brian asked Diccon about the Knight with the Red Shield, and Diccon said that while he had heard of him, as he had of Meliot's grave plight, he knew nothing about him. There was something in his look, however, that made Brian say, "Do not tell me that you have suffered at the hands of the Black Knight also."

"No," said Diccon. "But of late we have begun to fear that we may have as great an evil—or perhaps a worse one—in these parts."

"And what is that?"

"A few years ago an outlaw named Rufus, a great redheaded man, and two of his sons took refuge in the fens. Other like-minded ruffians joined them until he had a band of some fifteen or twenty. For some time now they have been raiding, robbing, and burning on the far side of the marshes. But within recent weeks men of his have been seen near here."

"And has naught been done about him?"

"Sir Roger of Reith, who lives south of the fens and from whom we hold our land, has gone looking for him several times. But the marshes are no place for knights on horseback, and even we who live so close to the fens are not sure exactly where Rufus's camp is." Then, seeing an anxious look on his wife's face, he added, "Not that we have anything to fear from him. Though we are all freemen in these parts, we are not rich enough to tempt him."

But while he spoke stoutly, it seemed to Brian that he was somewhat uneasy and he immediately began to talk of where they would sleep, offering his guests his own bed. Brian would have none of this, though, and it was finally agreed that they would sleep in the byre. Diccon came out with them and saw them comfortably settled in the hay of the loft before he retired.

Tertius had been strangely silent ever since they arrived at the stead, eating almost nothing, and Brian noticed that Maude had been watching him closely. When Brian questioned him, Tertius was short with him, saying that he was just tired. But when Brian woke during the night, he heard Tertius tossing and turning, and in the morning his eyes were dull and he was shaken by such chills that even when they covered him with their three cloaks, he still did not feel warm.

Brian reported this to Diccon and his wife, and they came out to the byre with him. By this time Tertius was flushed and hot instead of chilled.

"'Tis the ague or quartan fever," said Nan. "It is common in these parts. But I have a decoction that will help him."

"Of what do you make it?" asked Maude.

"Of feverfew," said Nan. "It is the best of medicines for fevers of all sorts."

"I have used it too," said Maude. "But I have always preferred elixir of willow bark."

"Oh?" said Nan with interest. "I have never tried that. Perhaps we should make some and give him both."

Again Diccon offered Tertius his own bed, but Tertius refused and, since the weather was warm and the loft airy, they agreed it might be better to leave him where he was.

"Don't look so worried," said Tertius when the two women had gone off together. "I'll live in spite of their medicines. Though I shouldn't joke about it because willow bark contains salicylic acid, which will help bring down a fever. In any case, as you can see, I won't lack good nursing."

In this Tertius was right, though it was principally Maude who took care of him, with a gentleness that was strangely at odds with her usual brusqueness: bringing him medicine and food and putting cool, wet cloths on his head when his fever rose. He was ill for more than a week. Then, as suddenly as it had come, the fever left him and, though he was quite weak, it was clear that he would soon be well.

"Is Tertius better today?" Amy asked Brian as they sat on a bench outside the farmhouse.

"Yes, he is," he answered. "He should be up and about in a day or so."

"I'm glad," she said. "I like him."

"More than you like me?" he asked teasingly, for he had spent much time with her while Tertius was ill.

"No," she said seriously. "But almost as much. And I like Maude, too."

"And we all love you, Amy. Though that's not surprising. Do you know what Amy means?"

"Of course. It means me."

"Well, yes," he said smiling. "But the name comes from the French, *aimé*, and it means someone who is very much loved."

"Oh," she said. "That's nice. How did they know about me?"

"Who?"

"The French."

"I'm afraid they don't. I'm afraid there are other Amys besides you."

"And other Brians and other Maudes?"

"Yes."

She thought about this for a moment. "Well, I still like all of you best." Then, "Is Maude very old?"

"Pretty old, I think. Why?"

"I just wondered. Sometimes she looks old and sometimes she doesn't."

Maude came out of the house at that moment with a bowl of soup for Tertius, and they both looked at her. It was true, Brian thought. Though she had spent many nights tending Tertius and looked tired, her face seemed less lined than it had and her hair less gray.

"What's wrong?" she asked. "Why are you staring at me that way?"

"Sorry," said Brian. "I didn't realize I was."

She frowned at them suspiciously, then went on to the byre.

"Perhaps," said Amy, "some people get younger every day instead of older."

"Perhaps," said Brian. "Shall we go for a ride on Gaillard?"

"Oh, yes!"

That evening as they sat about the fire after supper, Brian again studied Maude. Catching his eye, she scowled at him and he looked away, puzzled. For in the short space of that afternoon, it seemed to him that she had aged again and looked once more as she had when they first met.

The next day Maude let Tertius leave his bed and sit for a while in the sun and, by the end of the week, she pronounced him well enough to travel. When Brian looked questioningly at him, Tertius said, "I've been feeling well enough for several days now."

"In that case, we'll leave tomorrow."

"We'll miss you," said Nan. "All of you." For when Maude had not been tending Tertius, she had been with Nan; and, in spite of the great difference in their ages, they had become good friends.

It rained hard most of that day, but late in the afternoon it cleared. That evening Nan prepared a more lavish supper than usual for them, and they sat over it until quite late, eating nuts and fruit afterward and drinking homemade cider. They talked again about the Knight with the Red Shield, and Diccon suggested that they cross the fens and see whether Sir Roger knew anything about him. They also talked of Rufus and his outlaws who had been strangely quiet of late.

In the morning, Nan insisted on giving them meat, bread and cheese to add to their stock of provisions. Since there was something in

Diccon's eye that warned Brian against offering him money for this and his hospitality, he took the silver brooch from his cape and pinned it on Amy's dress.

"So that you will have something to remember us by," he explained.

"You will come see us again, won't you?" asked the child.

"Of course," said Brian.

She held up her arms to him and he kissed her and, when she had kissed Maude and Tertius also, they all mounted. Diccon accompanied them for a mile or so, for he was going to help a neighbor with his haying. After they had said good-bye to him, they continued on eastward along the edge of the marshes.

They were riding through rich bottom land, cut by dykes and ditches and with a few scattered farmsteads set on the higher ground to the north. Coming to a ditch that was wider than the others, they paused and glancing back, Brian stiffened.

"Look," he said, pointing.

There, far behind them, a column of smoke rose in the still morning air; smoke thicker and blacker than that of any hearth fire. They exchanged glances.

"You don't think . . . ?" began Brian.

Tertius had taken the spyglass from his saddlebag and was looking through it. When he lowered it, his face was pale.

"Yes," he said. "It's Diccon's farm."

Without a word, they turned their horses. Throwing the pack mule's leading rope to Tertius, Brian touched Gaillard with his heels and, with Maude close behind him, went galloping back the way they had come.

CHAPTER TWELVE

THEY HAD RIDDEN, slowly after they left Diccon, looking for the easiest way across the ditches and dykes because of the pack mule. But now, without the mule and with the black smoke rising ominously ahead of him, Brian rode as he had never ridden before; leaping the ditches and thundering across the meadows, constantly urging Gaillard on. And fast as Gaillard galloped, Maude on Gracielle kept pace with him.

They jumped the last ditch together and, looking ahead, saw what they had feared. The thatch of the farmhouse, still wet from the previous day's rain, smoldered in several places, sending up the thick column of smoke that had first caught Brian's eye. But the byre, with the dry hay in its loft, had burned fiercely and all that remained of it now were the charred fragments of its beams. As they rode through the meadow, Brian noticed that the cattle that usually grazed there were gone. Then they were at the house.

"Nan!" called Brian as he dismounted. "Amy!"

There was no answer, and they hurried inside. The larger, front room was empty, the benches and trestle table smashed. And the smaller room in back was empty too. Again Brian called. There was a distant, answering shout, and he and Maude went back outside.

Diccon, his face drawn, was running across the meadow toward them. Close behind him was an older, gray-haired man.

Reaching the house, Diccon looked at Brian and he nodded.

"They're gone," he said. "Your cattle, too. Was it Rufus?"

"Who else?" said Diccon. He turned to his companion.

"I'll rouse what men I can," said the older man. "Others will have seen the smoke too. And we'll do what we can." He started to go, then hesitated, looking at the smoldering thatch. "We can still save the house, Diccon."

"If Nan and Amy are gone, what care I about the house? Hurry, Andrew."

"I will," said the gray-haired man, and he ran off, back the way they had come. His face set and expressionless, Diccon went to the woodpile behind the house and picked up an axe. By the time he had returned, Tertius had come riding up, leading the pack mule.

"Rufus and his outlaws?" he asked.

"Yes," said Brian. "They took Nan and Amy as well as the cattle."

"Why?"

"They have taken women and children before," said Diccon grimly. "Sometimes for ransom, sometimes for other reasons. My friend

Andrew has gone to rouse our neighbors, but I shall not wait for them."

"You said you didn't know where Rufus's camp is," said Brian.

"I don't. But I'll find it."

"I'll go with you, of course. Tertius, you and Maude wait here, and . . ."

"No," said Tertius. "I'm coming too."

"But you've been ill . . ."

"We're both coming," said Maude. "We may not be much help, but we'll be some. Now stop wasting time."

Brian glanced at the two of them. "Very well," he said. "We'll take the horses as far as we can. Diccon, you ride with me."

He mounted Gaillard, helped Diccon up behind him, and they cantered down to the river and along it until they came to a place where the muddy bank showed many footprints, those of men as well as cattle.

"They must have crossed here," said Brian.

"Yes," said Diccon. "There's a ford here.

We'd better leave the horses."

They dismounted and tied the horses to a clump of willows. Brian took his shield from the saddle and they followed Diccon down the bank and into the river. The water was shallow, no deeper than Brian's waist, and there was a strip of firm ground on the other side. But beyond that, as far as the eye could see, were the fens; a green sea of sedge and reeds that grew tall as a man, dotted with open patches of marshy ground and pools of dark, stagnant water.

Diccon led the way across the further bank, with Brian and the others following. The ground was wet and soft, so soft that their feet sank into it an inch or two and, when they had passed, the mud filled their footprints, leaving no sign. But Brian, used to tracking game in the forest around Caercorbin, pointed to traces of mud on some of the clumps of marsh grass and Diccon said, "Yes. They came this way," and went on.

A marsh hawk flew overhead, giving its

sharp, wild cry as they crossed the open ground, and a bittern boomed in the distance. When they reached the first stand of sedge, there were further signs; the tall grass was bent and broken, and again there were the footprints of men and cattle in the firmer ground. They pressed through the rustling, swaying sedge, following the trail left by the passage of Rufus and his men. Midges, flies and other insects rose about them in clouds. On the far side of the sedge, Diccon paused. Ahead of them was another open place with a pool in its center, its surface covered with green scum. But the soft mud around it was flat and smooth with no sign of those who had gone before them.

"Now which way?" asked Brian.

"I don't know," said Diccon. "I have come this far before when I was hunting ducks, but I have never gone further."

"Is that smoke?" asked Maude, pointing.

Shading their eyes, Brian and Diccon peered across the marshes. Far off and somewhat to their left, beyond the pool and the sedge on its further side, patches of a darker green showed above the tall grass and reeds. And beyond them a few faint gray wisps drifted upward.

"It might be smoke or mist," said Diccon. "But since we have nothing else to guide us . . ."

He stepped forward into the mud and sank into it up to his ankles. He took another step and was up to his knees and still sinking. He turned, trying to go back, but could not pull his feet out of the clinging mud.

"Take my hand. Quickly!" said Brian. With Maude and Tertius holding him, he leaned forward and held out his hand. Diccon took it and, with great difficulty, they pulled him out of the quagmire and back to more solid ground.

"There must be some way to go on," said Diccon. "There must be! We know they came through here."

There was a faint rustling in the sedge to their right and a soft hiss. As they looked that way, the tall grass parted and a slim figure with long black hair appeared.

"Migbeg!" said Brian. "What are you doing here?"

Migbeg pointed back toward Diccon's stead and fluttered his hand upward.

"Smoke," said Maude. "You saw the smoke."

He nodded. Then, in pantomine, indicated a big man with a beard.

"Rufus," said Maude.

Again he nodded and, holding up both hands to show that the big man had ten men with him, he pointed to Diccon and made signs representing a woman and a child.

"Nan and Amy," said Maude. "We knew he had taken them. But where? Do you know where his camp is?" She sketched a shelter with her hands and looked at him questioningly.

Once more he nodded and, gesturing to them to follow him, he led them around the pool to the right, keeping to the firm ground on the edge of the rushes.

"I said I did not know what good it would do to have made him a friend," said Maude. "But I was wrong."

"Don't forget that Diccon is his friend, too," said Brian.

He had noticed that Migbeg carried a spear and that Sir Guy's sword was thrust through his belt. But happy as he was to have a guide through the fens, he could not help wishing that Migbeg were not alone but had brought his men with him.

Reaching the far side of the pool, Migbeg paused to make sure they were following him, then went on again. Through reed beds he led them, past other stagnant pools and around quaking patches of evil-smelling mud, always going south toward the heart of the marshes. Finally, coming to a stand of tall rushes, he stopped again. Holding his fingers to his lips, he worked his way through them so carefully that the reeds scarcely rustled. They went after him, trying to move as quietly as he did.

They came out on the bank of a clear stream.

Beyond it was an island of high ground. It was heavily wooded, and in the midst of it, shadowed by several swamp oaks, was an enclosure; a wall of posts with sharpened tops set closely together. Inside the palisade they could see the roofs of several crude huts. As they had hoped, Migbeg had led them to the outlaws' camp.

"Now what?" whispered Brian.

"Even if we can get inside," said Tertius, "I don't know what good it will do. There must be a dozen or more of them. Why don't you wait here, and I'll go back with Migbeg and get the others?"

"Wait?" growled Diccon. "Nan and Amy are in there!" And, axe in hand, he waded across the stream and started up toward the palisade.

"The two of you go back for the others," said Brian, "I can't let him go on alone." And he hurried after Diccon.

Together they circled the enclosure. There was a heavy gate set in one side of it. Touching Diccon on the shoulder, Brian pointed to it and to the thick wooden bar on the inside that held it closed. Diccon nodded.

"Stand back," he said, taking a firmer grip on his axe.

Hearing footsteps behind him, Brian turned and saw that, instead of going back to the farm, Maude, Tertius and Migbeg had followed them. He frowned at them, waving them away, but they ignored him.

Raising his axe high, Diccon brought it down between two of the posts, smashing the bar. Then he and Brian put their shoulders to the gate and pushed it open.

On the far side of the enclosure were the huts whose roofs they had seen from the outside. In a pen near the huts were Diccon's cattle, all except one. That one had been slaughtered and lay near the fire in the center of the camp. And gathered around it, watching a huge red-bearded man butcher it, were a dozen or more of the most villainous-looking ruffians Brian had ever seen.

The bloody knife still in his hand, the red-bearded man leaped to his feet.

"I've come for my wife and child, Rufus," said Diccon. "Where are they?"

Rufus looked at him with eyes like those of an angry boar. Then he threw back his head and laughed.

"You've come for them?" he said. "You?"

"Don't be a fool, Rufus!" said Tertius. "Do you think we'd come alone? Lay down your arms!" For several of the outlaws were reaching for their weapons. "Did you hear me? Lay them down! The camp is surrounded."

The outlaws looked around uneasily, and at that moment there was a faint rustling in the trees that overhung the palisade.

"He's lying!" said Rufus. "Who'd come here with them? They're alone."

Drawing swords and knives and hefting axes, the outlaws began to spread out and advance toward them.

"Wait!" said Rufus. "I've had no real sport

in weeks. I'll handle them myself. Beginning with you, farmer!" he said to Diccon.

"No," said Brian. "With me. By your leave, Diccon." And brushing past him, he strode to the center of the enclosure.

"Listen to him!" said Rufus. "Harken to our courtly young gentleman. By your leave, he says. Oh, I do like manners. Almost as much as I like spilling gentle blood!"

Thrusting the knife into his belt, he held out his hands. Two redheaded outlaws, younger than he and clearly his sons, stood just behind him. One of them handed him a buckler and the other a sword.

"I'll gut you like a herring!" roared Rufus. "I'll carve you like a Christmas goose!"

"I give you leave to try," said Brian, raising his shield and drawing Starflame.

"You give me leave?" whispered Rufus. "You give me . . . ?"

Bellowing, he heaved up his sword and charged at Brian, cutting down at him with a stroke that would have felled a tree.

Moving lightly, Brian slid away from it so smoothly that he barely needed his shield to fend it off. He knew he should be afraid. For while Rufus was not a skilled swordsman, he was a grown man, much bigger and stronger than Brian, and there was no doubt he meant to kill him. But apart from Brian's cold anger at the outlaw, there was something else, something he had felt the first time he drew Starflame: a strange strength that seemed to flow from the sword, a sense that the blade was alive and that with it in his hand no one could stand against him.

Recovering, Rufus struck again and again, Brian fending off every blow. Then he struck, straight and true, and so keen was Starflame that it cut through the buckler, shearing away most of the upper half of it. Rufus staggered back and for the first time, there was doubt—even fear—in his eyes. Catching himself, he slashed at Brian, a great swashing blow, and another and another. But always moving to his left, Brian caught them on his shield and put them aside. Then, when Rufus was raising his sword, Brian struck again, catching the outlaw's blade near its middle. There was a shattering sound and the blade shivered into fragments, leaving Rufus holding only the hilt. Once more Brian brought Starflame up.

"I yield! I yield!" gasped Rufus. "Take the cattle, the woman and the child, but spare me!"

"And your men?" asked Brian.

"No one will raise a hand against you!"

"Very well," said Brian, lowering his sword. "Where are they, his wife and child?"

"In that hut," said Rufus, pointing.

Brian and Diccon both started toward it. But as they walked past Rufus,

"Brian!" shouted Tertius.

"Look out!" shrieked Maude.

Glancing over his shoulder, Brian saw that Rufus had snatched the knife from his belt and was leaping after him to stab him in the back. But quickly as Rufus had moved, Migbeg was even quicker. His right hand flashed forward and Rufus stiffened. He stood there for a moment, looking down in surprise at the head of Migbeg's spear that stood out a handsbreadth from his chest. Then the knife dropped from his hand, his knees buckled and he fell forward on his face.

"Back to the others!" said Brian to Diccon.

He and Diccon ran back to where Maude, Tertius and Migbeg waited; Maude and Tertius with daggers in their hands, and Migbeg with the sword Brian had given him. But as the outlaws, howling with rage, charged toward them, more spears whistled out of the trees that overlooked the palisade, striking down both of Rufus's sons and killing or wounding several others. The remaining outlaws broke and fled out the gate. Dropping from the trees where they had been hiding, Migbeg's men ran after them as grimly and silently as wolves.

Brian watched them go, then turned to Tertius.

"How did you know they were there?" he asked him.

"I didn't," said Tertius.

"But you told Rufus the camp was surrounded."

"Desperate plights call for desperate sleights," said Tertius. "I hoped he'd believe it because I thought he'd think we were as mad to come here alone as I did."

"But still you followed us," said Brian. "And so did you, Maude. Why?"

"I have never known anyone," said Maude, "who could ask sillier questions than you. Let's see about Nan and Amy."

Diccon was already at the nearest hut. The door was closed and tied with withies. Cutting them with his axe, Diccon pulled the door open. The inside of the hut was dark, and at first they could see nothing.

"Nan!" said Diccon tentatively. "Amy!"

Two figures in the far corner stirred, and then they were both in his arms.

"Are you all right?" asked Diccon.

Nan, her face tear-stained, nodded.

"I was frightened," she said. "Terribly frightened. But I knew you'd come."

"So did I," said Amy. "And I knew you'd come too," she said to Brian.

"Did you, Amy?" he said kissing her. "Even though we were gone?"

"Yes," she said firmly. "Can we go home now? I don't like this place, and I didn't like those men."

"I don't think you or anyone else need ever worry about them again," said Brian.

By this time Migbeg had joined them and was standing just outside the hut.

"Who's that?" asked Amy, looking at him curiously.

"That's Migbeg," said Brian.

"Is he a friend of yours?"

"A very good friend," said Brian, "of mine, of your father's and of yours too. For without him we should never have found our way here.

Nor," looking past Migbeg at Rufus's body, "is it likely that any of us would have left here."

"Then I suppose I should thank him," said Amy. And smiling at him, she said, "Thank you, Migbeg."

Migbeg looked down at her gravely. Then something happened to his fierce, dark face and, for the first time since they had met him, he smiled too.

CHAPTER THIRTEEN

IT TOOK THEM a good deal longer to cross the marshes on their return than it had to get to the outlaws' camp. For, besides Nan, Amy and the cattle, they had three women with them: poor frightened creatures who had been captured by Rufus and his men in earlier raids south of the fens. In the same hut was the booty the outlaws had brought back from those raids: goblets, candlesticks, a few pieces of jewelry and a small bag of coins. Brian and the others had wanted none of this and told Diccon to keep it, but he said he would keep only enough to pay for the rebuilding of his house and byre and would give the rest to Sir Roger to share among those who had suffered at the outlaws' hands.

As they neared the river, they heard voices and there, crossing at the ford, were Andrew and some two dozen farmers; a few armed with swords, the rest with bows, pikes and axes.

Seeing Nan and Amy, Andrew's bright eyes went to Migbeg and his men who were still with them, guiding them and helping them drive the cattle.

"It seems you have other friends besides us, Diccon," he said. Then, looking again at Nan and Amy, "They are all right?"

"Yes."

"What of Rufus?"

"He and his sons are dead. As for the others, I don't think we need worry about them again."

"That's good news. And I have news for you that is almost as good. We were able to save your house. The roof will need thatching, but we will help you with that and also help you build a new byre. So things are not as bad as they might have been, thanks to your friends."

"Thanks indeed," said Diccon.

Uneasy in the presence of all these strangers, Migbeg's men drew back to the edge of the river. Only Migbeg himself stood his ground. Going over to him, Diccon took his hand and told him he would never forget what he had done and that he hoped that one day he would be able to repay him. Migbeg may not have understood the words, but it was clear that he understood what lay behind them for he nodded gravely. As he turned to go, Maude stopped him.

"Wait, Migbeg," she said. "Brian gave you something before: that sword. But without your help we would not be here now, and so I would like to give you something too."

Reaching up inside her sleeve, she took a gold bracelet from her arm and slipped it onto his. He looked down at it, at her, and then—as he had with Brian—he put his left hand on her shoulder and gripped her wrist with his right. Again as he had with Brian, he looked deep into her eyes. Then raising his spear in salute, he led his men across the river and back toward the heath.

As Andrew had said, except for the partly burned thatch, Diccon's house was undamaged. And since it was late afternoon, Brian, Maude and Tertius spent the night there.

"Will you *still* come see us again?" asked Amy the next morning as they got ready to leave.

"Yes, Amy," said Brian.

"All of you?"

"I can't speak for Maude and Tertius. They may not be able to. But I shall come back."

She was sitting on his lap, holding his hand and playing with his ring. Looking down at it she asked, "What's this? The animal on your ring?"

"It's a wivern," he said. "The Caercorbin crest."

"What's a wivern?"

"It's a kind of dragon with wings and a long tail."

"Oh," she said, examining it. "It's different from our dragon. Our dragon has horns."

Brian looked at her, then at Diccon.

"Is that true?" he asked. "Is there a dragon in these parts?"

"So they say," said Diccon. "I have never seen it, but my grandfather said that he did once—in the hills south of the fens."

"And it has horns?"

"So he said."

Again they said farewell, and Diccon repeated everything he had said to Migbeg—that he would never forget what they had done—and this time Nan as well as Amy kissed them all and both of them stood with Diccon, waving to them as they rode off eastward along the river.

"Now where?" asked Maude.

"I suspect we are all thinking the same thing," said Tertius.

"About the dragon's horn," said Brian. "That the Knight with the Red Shield will have drunk from it."

"Yes," said Tertius. "Not that I believe there is such a thing as a dragon."

"Even if there is," said Maude, "I don't see what good it will do. I mean, if it's alive how can anyone drink from its horn?"

"I don't know," said Tertius. "But since it's the only clue we have at the moment, I think we should follow it."

Brian glanced at Maude and when she shrugged, he said, "Then we'll go south. I've always wanted to see a dragon."

They continued on along the riverbank until they came to a causeway that led south across the fens. It was old and narrow, turning and twisting this way and that, linking together the occasional islands of solid ground. They rode along it for most of the day, meeting no one and seeing nothing but marsh birds: geese, ducks, herons and an occasional hawk. Late in the afternoon they reached the far side of the fens, and to the south they could see the hills. They rode toward them, finding them to be higher than they had seemed and quite rocky and barren. There, too, they met no one. But just before dusk, when they were looking for a place to camp, they came to a valley that was surrounded by steep cliffs. A stream ran through it and, sitting at the mouth of a cave at the base of the cliffs, was a hermit.

He was a small man, his face as brown and wrinkled as a walnut. He wore a ragged, faded robe with a cowl. Birds circled around his head and perched on his shoulders. He glanced at them as they approached, then pointedly turned his back to them.

"Good evening," said Brian politely.

His back still to them, the hermit grunted.

"Are we disturbing you?" asked Brian.

"Of course you're disturbing me," he said, brushing the birds off his shoulders.

"I'm sorry. We'll go away, then."

"Since you're here," he said gruffly, "obviously you've got to stay. But don't expect me to entertain you." And rising, he disappeared into the cave.

"What shall we do?" asked Brian.

"You heard him," said Maude. "He couldn't say so, but it's clear he wants us to stay."

Unsaddling the horses and the mule, they turned them loose to graze on the grass that grew along the banks of the stream and built a fire. While they were eating their supper the hermit came out of the cave again.

"Is that cheese?" he asked.

"Yes, it is," said Tertius. "Would you like some?"

The hermit fixed him with a fierce blue eye.

"Like some? When I first came here I used to dream about cheese. Not about a soft bed or a warm room or any other kind of food, but just cheese. And now you're tempting me again to the sin of gluttony!"

"I don't see," said Maude, "how eating one piece of cheese can be called gluttony. Here." And cutting a large wedge of it she set it down in front of him.

He looked at it, at her, then, "But suppose,

after I eat it, I want another piece?"

"If you do, you can have it," she said. "But resisting temptation is a recognized form of spiritual exercise."

He continued to look at the cheese and finally, with a sigh, he picked it up and began to eat it. The birds were back, circling his head and settling on his shoulders and now he gave up pretending to brush them away and instead held up bits of cheese which they took from his fingers. When he had finished, he sighed again.

"Now I suppose I'll start dreaming about it again," he said. "But I don't care. I suppose you're on a quest."

"Yes," said Brian. "Or rather on three different quests."

"Are you sure?"

"What do you mean?"

"In the end, most quests turn out to be the same one. Isn't that so?" he asked Tertius.

"I know that there are those who think so," said Tertius. "And whether it's true or not, I've felt from the beginning that our three quests are intertwined."

"And what's yours?"

"I'm looking for someone to teach me something."

"Something meaning anything at all or something in particular?"

"Something in particular. But Brian here is looking for something even more specific: the Knight with the Red Shield. Do you know anything about him? Have you ever seen him or heard of him?"

"No," said the hermit. "You're the first visitors I've had in months. What about your quest?" he asked Maude.

"I'd rather not talk about it," she said.

"Why not?"

"Because I don't want to. But perhaps you can tell us something about the dragon."

"What dragon?"

"We were told that there was one somewhere in these hills. Is that true?"

"Yes. He lives in one of the valleys to the south."

"What kind of dragon is he?" asked Brian.

"What kind?"

"Yes. Is he wicked?"

"There you go," said the hermit irascibly, "tempting me. A question like that is an open invitation to a homily on good and evil, on man's nature and the nature of beasts. And I hate that sort of thing. Don't you?"

"Yes," said Brian.

"Then let me just say that, as far as I know, he has never hurt anyone or anything."

"In other words, he's not dangerous."

"Ah," said the hermit. "That's something else again. I'm sure he could be. Why are you so interested in him?"

"Because we thought we'd like to see him."

"Does he have anything to do with your quest?"

"Yes."

"Then of course you must see him. I'll tell

you how to find him tomorrow."

They slept beside the fire outside the cave that night and in the morning when they had breakfasted and saddled up, the hermit said, "You wanted to know about the dragon."

"Yes," said Brian.

"Continue straight on south. He lives in the next valley but one. You can't miss it." He paused. "Now I suppose you'd like me to do something that one expects of hermits: either bless you or give you some truly sage advice. But the truth is that I'm not holy enough for the one or wise enough for the other."

"I don't believe that," said Brian politely.

"Well, you should. Everyone thinks that because a man's a hermit there must be something special about him. But, in my case at least, there's not. Still," looking thoughtfully at Brian, "since you're the warrior of your little group, perhaps there's something I can say to you. Remember that refusing a challenge can be as much of a test as accepting one."

"I'm not sure I know what that means," said Brian, "but I'll remember it. Good-bye."

"Good-bye," said the hermit.

They mounted and rode on south. The next valley was rocky and barren too, much like the one they had just left. But when they came to the one beyond that, they found it to be quite different. It too was surrounded by cliffs, but it was large and green, partly meadow and partly wooded, with a clear blue lake in its center. The trail that led down into it was so steep and narrow they had to dismount and lead their horses.

It was almost noon, and as they rode across the meadow toward the wood that bordered the lake, the heat was almost tropical.

"I've been thinking about what you said yesterday, Maude," said Tertius. "About not seeing what good it would do to look for the dragon. And it occurred to me that if we had one of its horns, we would not have to go on searching for the Knight with the Red Shield. He would have to find us. I mean, dragons' horns aren't exactly common."

"That isn't precisely what I said," said Maude. "I said I didn't see how anyone could drink from its horn while it was still alive."

"Obviously we'd have to kill it," said Tertius. "But before we can do that we have to find it."

"That shouldn't be too difficult," said Brian. "Wouldn't it live in a cave in one of the cliffs?"

"I've no idea," said Tertius. "I told you I don't believe there is such a thing."

"What about Saint George?" asked Brian.

"I always thought that what he fought was a crocodile."

"Do you mean a cockadrill serpent?"

"It's been called that, but actually it's a large reptile that lives in Africa. Only of course it doesn't have horns."

They were in the wood now, riding toward the lake. Suddenly Gaillard tossed his head and snorted and, almost as if it were in answer, they heard a deep rumbling sound ahead of them, followed by a loud splashing. Raising his hand in warning, Brian checked Gaillard and they dismounted. Tying the horses and the mule to trees, they began working their way through the thick underbrush. When they reached the edge of the wood, Brian carefully parted the fronds of tall fern and peered out.

And there, some forty or fifty yards away, was the dragon.

It was not at all what Brian had expected. It was not scaly, did not have wings or claws, and did not breathe fire. But it was still the largest and most frightening-looking creature he had ever seen.

It stood at least twice as high and was more than twice as long as a bull. Its skin was gray and wrinkled, and its tail was heavy and so long that it trailed on tile ground. But the strangest part of it was its head, which was enormous, almost a third the side of its body. It had three horns; two projecting forward menacingly from above its eyes and a third one rising from its nose. Its whole head seemed to be armored, and a frill of bone extended out from the back of it like some curious neckguard.

Brian heard Tertius gasp and turned to look at him.

"I said I didn't believe there was such a thing," whispered Tertius, "and I still don't. It's a triceratops."

"What's that?"

"A dinosaur, one of the ornithiscians. They've supposedly been extinct for thousands of years."

"Well, this one isn't," said Maude. "It's here, waiting for our dragon slayer." Then to Brian, "What are you going to do about it?"

"I'm not sure yet," said Brian.

As soon as he had seen the monster, he had drawn Starflame. The huge creature was not going to be easy to deal with. Arrows would be useless against it: it was so big that they would seem no more than pinpricks. The best way to kill it would have been on horseback with a lance as Saint George had done with his dragon. But Brian did not have a lance. That left his sword. And though he knew he would have to move quickly to avoid the beast's horns, he was convinced he could do so.

Tense and excited, but curiously unafraid, he stood up. And as he picked out the place where he would drive Starflame home, the monster turned. It had been standing knee-deep in the lake, drinking. Now, rumbling and wheezing deep in its chest, it splashed back to shore and came toward them. It moved slowly, heavily, almost painfully. And as it plodded along the bank with its great horned head swinging from side to side, they could see that its small eyes were dull and rheumy.

"I think it's blind," said Brian.

"Not quite, but almost," said Tertius. "It's very old."

"All the better for you, Brian," said Maude.

"No, it's not," said Brian. It was almost

opposite them now, still moving slowly, still wheezing plaintively. "I'm not going to kill it."

"Why not?"

"Because I can't. It's practically helpless."

"Step out there and show yourself and you'll see how helpless it is."

"It doesn't matter. I still can't do it."

"What about your quest?"

"Perhaps we can find another one who's younger and fiercer and really doing harm, devastating the land."

"And to whom they sacrifice beautiful maidens. Then you can rescue her and live happily ever after."

"Please don't, Maude," said Brian unhappily. "I'm probably not a good knight errant or a good quester, but I just can't do it."

"Then that's that," said Maude. "Somehow I don't think there is another one. I have a feeling he's the last dragon in the world. You're sure you don't want the glory of killing it?"

"Yes."

"I'm glad," said Tertius.

At that moment, as if it had been in pain of some sort but now felt better, the great horned monster picked up its head and began moving faster, almost gamboling on the grassy margin of the lake. And while, because of its size, there was something ludicrous about its behavior, there was also something infinitely touching about it.

Out of the corner of his eye, Brian saw Maude's face soften. They watched the dragon until it disappeared into the wood on the far side of the lake. Then, mounting their horses, they went back the way they had come.

CHAPTER FOURTEEN

THEY PAUSED WHEN they reached the head of the valley. They were on a ridge that ran north and south with the dragon's valley on one side of them and the hermit's on the other. Brian was curiously reluctant to retrace his steps and Maude and Tertius admitted that they were too.

"Then which way shall we go?" asked Brian. "North or south?"

"I don't know," said Tertius. "You decide, Maude."

"Very well."

Riding a short distance away, she sat with her back to them as if waiting for something. Suddenly, far above them in the almost cloudless sky, a black dot appeared. With wings folded, it dropped down toward them. When it was just over their heads, its wings opened and they could see that it was that smallest of falcons, a merlin. It circled around them once, twice, so close that they could see its hooked beak and fierce round eyes. Then, straight as an arrow, it flew toward the South. Without a word, they turned their horses and rode after it.

They rode south for several days, through windswept uplands where deer bounded off with long, effortless leaps as they approached, then paused to watch them as they passed. As they came down off the high ground, the heather, furze and bracken gave way first to pines and then to oaks and beeches. The fourth day after leaving the dragon's valley, the forest began to open up and the track that they were following became a road that wound through fields and meadows where sheep and cattle grazed. At about noon they heard hammering and, rounding a bend, they found themselves at a fork. The road they were on went down a hill to a small village, while a path branched off to the left toward the crest of the hill. Standing at the fork and nailing a sign to a weathered post was a man who seemed strangely out of place there.

He was small, dark and sharp-featured. And though his clothes were dusty and somewhat worn, they were those of a townsman rather than a countryman. Seeing them, he took off his cap with a flourish and bowed, saying, "A very good day to you, gentles."

They returned his greeting and paused to read the sign he had just put up. It pointed to the left and it read:

THIS WAY TO THE GIANT.

SINGLE COMBATS AT ANY HOUR OF

THE DAY OR NIGHT.

THIS WAY TO THE WITCH.

FORTUNES TOLD. ALSO SPELLS, CHARMS,

AND CURSES.

"Is he really a giant?" asked Brian.

"He is indeed," said the man.

"And is he dangerous?"

"There have been no complaints about him that I know of," said the man carefully.

"About his being dangerous or not dangerous?"

"Both," said the man. "Or either, as the case may be."

"What about the witch?" asked Tertius.

"She is said to be his sister," said the man. "A very interesting family."

"Would you like to see her?" Brian asked Tertius. "I know that what you were looking for was a magician, but . . ."

"I don't know," said Tertius. "It sounds a little commercial to me."

"Are you talking about the sign?" asked the man. "Do you think it should be phrased differently?"

"I don't think there should be any sign at all. Exactly who are you?"

"The name's David," said the man, bowing

again. "David ap David. Welsh, of course. Formerly a scribe and chronicler, one of the most eminent chroniclers in Camelot."

"What did you chronicle?" asked Brian.

"The gestes, deeds and exploits of the knights," said David ap David. "When they returned from a quest, I would take down the tale of their adventures. As you'd suspect, their accounts were often surprisingly similar and sometimes a little dull. So, in putting them into their final form, I would do a certain amount of polishing and embroidering. And," he coughed discreetly, "in certain cases I would arrange to have them turned into chansons or ballads."

"You're not a chronicler," said Tertius. "You're a premature p.r."

"I beg your pardon?"

"A public relations man."

"I'm afraid I've never heard that term."

"You seem to have managed well enough in spite of it," said Tertius. "But what are you doing here?"

"Well, you know how things are at Camelot right now—practically nothing happening—so I thought I'd travel around a bit, see what I could do elsewhere. When I got here, I found the whole shire was in a very bad way."

"Bad how?"

"Very poor crops this year. The obvious thing to do was to attract questers. And though this is off the beaten track, I thought it could be done. I told the locals what had happened elsewhere, how there are dozens of knights riding west every week to take a whack at that villain, Sir Bruce Sans Pité, because I'd described his nefarious deeds in several of my chronicles. And almost as many going north after Sir Seferides and Sir Palomides."

"Are they villains too?" asked Brian.

"Well, they're Saracens," said David.

"What about the giant and his sister?" asked Maude.

"What makes them villains?"

"Why, I don't know that they are," said

David. "But apparently he is a giant, and . . ." He broke off, for Maude was looking at him coldly and with obvious distaste. "Beg pardon, ma'am, but are *you* a witch?"

"Of course she's not," said Brian.

"Don't be too sure," said Maude. Then to David, "Have you seen them yourself?"

"The giant and his sister! No. It didn't seem necessary. I mean, the locals have told me all about them, and . . ."

"I think you should see them," said Maude. "With us."

"But . . ." Then, as Maude continued to look at him, "Just as you say, ma'am."

He mounted his horse, a dispirited jade that was grazing at the side of the road, and followed them along the path to the left. They halted when they reached the crest of the hill. Below them, in a hollow, was a cottage that, at first glance, seemed no different from any other. It was only when Brian looked at it closely that he realized the door was some ten or twelve feet high.

Though smoke rose from the chimney, there was no one in sight. But as they started down into the hollow, David ap David's horse snorted and, almost at once, the giant appeared from behind the cottage.

Like the cottage, at first glance there did not seem to be anything strange or different about him: he looked like an ordinary farmer in low boots and a tunic belted at the waist. It was only when Brian saw that it was not a cat or a small dog he carried under his arm but a full-grown sheep that he realized the man was almost twice as tall as other men.

The giant stood there for a moment, looking at them. Then, dropping the sheep, he picked up an enormous club.

"Lamorna!" he called, his eyes on Brian. "Here's another one!"

Tertius had been studying him; his craggy features, large head and protruding jaw.

"Acromegaly," he said. "A pituitary type."

"What's that mean?" asked Brian.

"An overactive pituitary gland."

"But he's a real giant."

"Oh, yes. There's no doubt about that."

Now the cottage door opened and a woman hurried out. Though she carried a broom, she did not look at all like a witch, for she was plump and pleasant looking. And while she was of average height, standing next to her giant brother she seemed no bigger than a child.

"Who are you?" she asked. "And what do you want?"

"We're travelers," said Maude. "And we just wanted to see you, talk to you."

"You're a knight, aren't you?" said the giant to Brian.

"No. A squire."

"That's just as bad," said the giant, his club poised, "if not worse. You come here with those great big spears of yours and the next thing I know . . ."

"But I haven't got a spear," said Brian.

"That's true," said the giant. "But you've got

a sword, and . . . you mean you don't want to fight me?"

"No. Why should I?"

"I don't know," said the giant. "But then I don't understand what's been happening here lately either. We were born here, Lamorna and I," he explained earnestly and a little plaintively, "and everyone in these parts knows us. Whenever they need help with something, lifting a roof beam, pulling a cow from a bog or dragging a rock from a field, they call on me. 'Get Giles,' they say. We never had any trouble with them. Then, a few days ago, strangers started coming here."

"Knights," said his sister. "All in armor. They'd gawk at Giles as if he were some sort of monster and then, as he said, they'd come riding at him with those great long spears."

"And what happened?" asked Tertius.

"The first one took me by surprise and almost stuck me," said Giles. "But I knocked him off his horse and threw him in the ditch. I was ready for the next one and the ones after that, served them the same way. And those I didn't take care of, Lamorna did. Right handy with her broom she is."

"What I can't understand," said Lamorna, "is how it all began, why it's happening."

"We can tell you that," said Maude. "Well?" she said, fixing David ap David with an icy stare.

"I meant no harm by it," he said awkwardly. "I was thinking about the others, the locals."

"You mean he had something to do with it?" said Giles. "What?"

"I just put up a few signs," said David. Then as Giles and Lamorna as well as Maude looked at him he added, "There's nothing to get upset about. I'll take them down again. At least . . . Could I leave up just one or two?"

"No!" said Maude.

"All right, all right. I'll go take care of them right away. But I'd like to come back afterward and talk to you," he said to Giles.

"About what?"

"A proposal that might put some silver in both our purses. There aren't all that many giants around, you know. Not real ones. And since the magnates are always looking for something new and different to bring jousters to their tourneys, I thought I might take you over to the one they're holding at Belvoir next week. We could put you up against, say, half a dozen knights . . ."

Giles had been leaning on his club while they talked. Now, with a sudden roar, he raised it high and ran toward David ap David. His face pale, the little man turned his horse and went galloping away up the hill.

"Giles!" called Lamorna sharply as the giant started after him.

"I'm sorry," he said, coming back. "If there's one thing I hate, it's violence. But there was something about that man. . . ."

"Don't apologize," said Maude. "The only

thing *I'm* sorry about is that you didn't catch him."

"Then he isn't a friend of yours?"

"We only met him a short while ago," said Brian, "putting up one of his signs. If he doesn't take it down, we will."

"I'm very grateful to you," said Giles, but he added anxiously, "Are you sure you don't want to fight? As I said, I hate violence. But if it's important to you . . . I mean, if you've taken a vow or are on a quest of some sort . . ."

"I am on a quest," said Brian. "But it has nothing to do with fighting giants."

"I'm delighted to hear that," said Giles, relaxing. "In that case, you must come in and have a little something with us."

"It's very kind of you," said Brian. "But . . ."

"I insist," said Giles. "Lamorna baked some pasties this morning. She makes very good pasties."

"These should be good," said Lamorna, "now that turnips are in. This way."

Dismounting, they followed the giant and his sister into the cottage. They found themselves in a curious room for, while the table and benches were of normal size, there was one chair in it that was so huge it made everything else seem as if it had been made for children. While Lamorna bustled about warming up the pasties, Giles poured out ale for them. He gave Maude and Tertius tankards.

"You must drink from this," he said to Brian, handing him an enormous drinking horn. "It's something we keep for honored guests, and it will bring you good fortune."

Though he took it with both hands, it was so heavy that Brian could barely lift it. But, toasting the giant, he drank long and deeply from it, then lowered it and looked at it. It was almost four feet long and like no horn he had ever seen before. For while it was white as ivory, it was not curved but straight and had a spiral running around it from its pointed tip to the silver mounting of its rim.

Tertius had been looking at it too.

"It's a narwhale's tusk," he said.

"Is it?" said Giles. "That's very interesting. It's been in the family for generations, and we've never been sure what it was. We've always called it the dragon's horn."

Maude had been talking to Lamorna. Now she broke off, and she and Tertius exchanged glances with Brian.

"The dragon's horn?" said Brian.

"Yes."

"Has anyone else drunk from it recently?"

"Why, yes," said Giles. "It's strange that you should ask that, for we haven't used it for years. But a knight came through here a week or so ago, just before all the trouble started. He had been riding hard, was very hot and thirsty, and since he was the first visitor we'd had in some time, I gave it to him to drink from also."

"Do you know his name?"

"No," said Giles. "I never asked, and he never told us. But he was a very gallant knight."

"Did he, by any chance, carry a red shield?"

"Why, yes," said Giles. "Now that you mention it, he did."

"Are you sure about that?" asked Lamorna.

"Of course I'm sure," said Giles. Then, as Brian looked again at Maude and Tertius, "Do you know him?"

"No, but I've been looking for him. In fact, that's my quest. Do you have any idea where he was going, where I could find him?"

"Yes," said Giles. "He was going home. He said he had not been there in more than ten years, but he had heard there was trouble there."

"Trouble?"

"Something to do with one of his female relatives. His cousin, I believe."

"She was in some kind of danger?"

"No. I think she was making the trouble, up to some kind of mischief."

"Oh," said Brian. "Do you know where it is? His home, I mean."

"Well, when he left here he rode that

way," said Giles, pointing southwest. "But I'm afraid . . ."

"I know a bit more than that," said Lamorna. "I asked him if it was a long journey, and he said it was. That his castle was the last one in England."

"The last one?"

"I think he meant that there was nothing beyond it but the sea."

"Thank you," said Brian, handing the great drinking horn back to the giant. "If you don't mind, I think . . ."

"But you can't go yet," said Lamorna. "You haven't had your pasties." And she set them on the table.

They were golden brown, the crust light and flaky; and, impatient though he now was to be off, Brian finished his to the last crumb.

"I wish you did not have to leave," said Giles as they mounted their horses. "And more important, I wish there was something I could do to help you."

"You have," Brian assured him. "For the first time, we know where we must go."

"Really? I'm glad. And I hope your quest is successful."

"It will be," said Lamorna. "Though perhaps not in the way he thinks."

"She's always saying things like that," said Giles. "And she's usually right. It's what makes people think that she's a witch."

"Which of course is nonsense," said Lamorna. "It's only common sense. You're a determined and very likable young man," she told Brian, "so why shouldn't you be successful?"

"But why won't it be in the way I think?"

"Because that's the way quests are. We rarely find what we expected. Or, if we do, we find it in an unexpected place. Isn't that true?" she asked Tertius.

"I suspect it is," he said. "Not that I've done much thinking about it."

"Haven't you? I have the feeling that you've done a lot of thinking about a great many things.

And that's why your quest will be successful, too. As for you, my dear," she said to Maude. Then, as Maude looked at her fixedly, "Oh. Very well. If women don't keep one another's secrets, who will?"

"Will we see them again?" asked Giles.

"We'll make it our business to," said Lamorna.

"Then that's that," said Giles. "Good-bye for now."

"Good-bye," said Brian.

Maude had already turned her horse and was riding back up the hill, and as Brian followed her he wondered unhappily why it was that everyone seemed to know things he didn't. How did Lamorna for instance, not only know that Maude had a secret but apparently what it was? He, who had been with Maude for weeks, knew little more about her now than he had when they had first met.

They rode southwest all afternoon, halting at dusk in a clearing near the bank of a stream.

They built a fire and while Brian and Tertius unsaddled the horses, Maude went to the stream to get some water. Brian was examining Gaillard's hoofs when something—not a noise, but rather a sudden silence—made him look up. Maude, rigid, was standing on the far side of the clearing. And facing her, not a dozen yards away, was an enormous black boar.

For a moment they all stood frozen: Maude, Brian, Tertius and the boar. Then, as Brian drew Starflame, the boar charged.

Waiting until he was almost upon her, Maude dodged, twisting sideways away from him. And as she did, her feet slipped on the dry leaves and she fell heavily. The boar missed her by inches, turned with surprising speed and paused again, its head held low, its white tusks gleaming.

"Ho!" called Brian, running toward it. "Here!"

The boar hesitated, its red eyes going from Maude, now on her knees, to Brian.

"Here, I say!" shouted Brian, stamping his foot. Responding to his shout or to his movements the boar charged again; this time not at Maude, but at Brian.

Poised and sword in hand, Brian waited for it. He had been boar hunting several times with Sir Guy and, though he had never killed one of the great beasts himself, he knew how it should be done: the butt of the spear held firmly against the ground, the point presented so that the charging animal impaled himself on it. But he did not have a spear.

The boar was almost upon him now, so close that he could see the coarse bristles erect on its back and smell its rank, sour smell. Then, as it drove at him, he pivoted on the balls of his feet, swinging sideways out of its path and bringing Starflame down on its neck.

Something sharp ripped across his thighs and, like Maude, he went down. When he struggled to his feet, the boar was lying dead a few yards away from him, its tusks half-buried in the forest mold, and Maude was looking from it to him.

"Why did you do that?" she asked angrily.

"Do what?"

"Call him that way!"

"Why? Because he was about to charge again. You might have been killed."

"What about you?"

"Me?"

"Yes. What if *you* had been killed? Does that precious quest of yours mean so little to you?"

"No. No, of course not. It means a great deal to me. But . . ."

"You're a fool!" she said fiercely. And leaving him standing there with the blood from his wounds trickling down his legs, she walked off into the forest.

CHAPTER FIFTEEN

BRIAN'S WOUNDS were not as deep as they looked. While Tertius was helping him wash away the blood, Maude returned from the forest. Shouldering Tertius aside, she examined the twin slashes, spread an ointment on them, and bound them with strips of linen that she tore from the bottom of her shift.

Though the wounds were not serious, they were painful, and Brian did not sleep well that night. But in spite of that—and in spite of Maude's and Tertius's misgivings—they made an early start the next morning and put in a long day in the saddle. They camped that night in a meadow. While they were eating, Brian saw

Maude stiffen and begin going through her clothes. Then, rising, she went over to her saddlebags and began looking through them.

"Is anything wrong?" he asked. "Have you lost something?"

"Yes. A pouch."

"What kind of pouch?"

"What difference does it make?"

"I just thought . . . could you have lost it yesterday when you fell dodging the boar?"

"It's possible."

"Was there anything valuable or important in it? If there was, I could go back for it."

"A full day's ride? Don't be ridiculous."

"What's ridiculous about it? And why are you being so surly? I'm just trying to help."

"When I want your help, I'll ask for it."

"Very well," said Brian, annoyed. "I'll remember that."

He was still annoyed the next morning, and his irritation was increased by Maude's behavior. For she said hardly a word to him, rode behind him when they started out and kept to herself, on her own side of the fire when they camped at night.

For almost two weeks they rode south and west, at first through open farmland and then through forests and across chalky downs, coming at last to the coast where cliffs dropped sheer to the sea. Now the weather worsened. The wind shifted to the north and for several days it rained; a cold, steady rain that chilled them to the bone. When the rain ceased, thick fog rolled in from the sea and this was even worse, for they could ride only at a slow walk, picking their way through the murk. Then, just before dusk, the fog lifted and that evening, for the first time in many nights, they could see the stars and their fire seemed to have some warmth.

As was her custom, Maude sat on the far side of the fire and looking at her in the ruddy glow of the embers, it seemed to Brian that once again—as at Diccon's—a change had come over her.

Instead of looking drawn, tired and older after so much cold and discomfort, she looked younger. Putting it down to a trick of the light, he rolled himself in his cloak and went to sleep. But in the morning, when the sun was up, he studied her again. She had thrown back her hood while she ate, and her eyes were clearer, her face less lined and her hair less gray than he remembered.

"Do you think it's possible for people to change?" he asked Tertius when she had gone off to saddle her horse.

"Not only possible, but inevitable," said Tertius. "Our bodies supposedly renew themselves every seven years. What sort of change did you have in mind?"

"It wasn't anything I had in mind. It's Maude. Does she look different to you?"

"Different how?"

"I know it's impossible, but . . . younger, less unattractive."

Putting on his spectacles, Tertius looked at him thoughtfully.

"Why do you think it's impossible?"

"You mean it isn't?"

"You know what they say about beauty, don't you?"

"No."

"As a matter of fact, they say several things. That it's only skin deep and that it lies in the eye of the beholder. In other words, perhaps it's you who are changing, not she."

"Why not? Stranger things than that have happened." And rising, he went off to saddle his palfrey.

They rode on, keeping the sea always on their left. And now, though the days were getting shorter—for they were well into autumn—the sun shone more brightly than ever in the clear sky and it was as warm as early summer was in the north. Day after day they went on, through rolling country high above a deep blue sea where gulls and terns circled and soared and cormorants nested on the rocky islands offshore.

Though the land through which they were

traveling seemed fertile, the few farms they passed were abandoned, and they met no one whom they could question. Then, late one afternoon, they came to a headland, a rocky promontory that jutted out into the sea. As they drew near it, they saw that there was a castle at its tip, the sea on three sides of it. And they also saw that there was nothing beyond it, that at this point the coast no longer continued on to the south or west, but ran north.

Remembering what Lamorna had said, Brian checked Gaillard and glanced at Tertius.

"Yes," said Tertius. "I suppose you could call it the last castle in England. So it could well be what we've been looking for."

"I'm sure it is," said Maude, "and I don't like it."

"Why?" asked Brian.

She shrugged without answering. They were on a hill on the landward side of the peninsula, surrounded by furze, bracken and huge gray rocks. Maude looked about.

"There's someone there," she said, "watching us."

Turning, Brian saw something move near the base of one of the rocks.

"Come out," he called, sensing that the figure crouched there in fear rather than menace. "Come out. We won't hurt you."

Slowly the figure rose, a dark-haired man in ragged clothes. He came no nearer but stood where he was, a dozen yards away, waist-deep in the bracken.

"We're looking for the Knight with the Red Shield," said Brian. "Do you know him?"

Watching him warily, the man shook his head.

"You're sure?"

The man nodded.

"Then whose castle is that?"

"Whose is everything in these parts?" said the man in a harsh, rasping voice. "Hers, the Dark Lady's."

"The Dark Lady?" Again Brian glanced at Tertius.

"Don't forget why he was going home," said Tertius. "Because of his cousin."

"You're right," said Brian, turning again to the black-haired man. "Thank you."

"You're going there, to the castle?" asked the man.

"Yes," said Brian. "Why?"

Throwing back his head, the man laughed, a shrill, high-pitched laugh as wild as the calling of the gulls.

"Stop that!" said Maude sharply. "Why shouldn't we go there?"

The man stopped laughing and looked at her anxiously. Then, as she edged Gracielle toward him, he turned, dived into the bracken and disappeared.

"Somehow I get the impression," said Tertius, "that this Dark Lady is not well liked around here."

"And of course you think we should find out

why," said Maude dryly.

"It's not up to me. It's your quest, Brian. What do you say?"

"After coming so far, I'm certainly not going to turn back now," said Brian. "But the two of you needn't come with me."

"Quite true," said Maude. Then, as he hesitated, "What are you waiting for?"

"If you're *not* coming," said Brian awkwardly, "I wanted to say good-bye."

They both looked at him, Maude with some irritation and Tertius with amused affection.

"In case you've forgotten," he said, "we've come just as far as you have. Let's go."

They rode down the hill and out onto the peninsula. The castle was farther away than it had seemed, and it was almost dusk before they were close enough to it to see it clearly. The bailey wall ran across the neck of the peninsula with a deep dry moat before it, these and the steep cliffs dropping to the sea on the other three sides making it almost impregnable.

They drew rein, studying it. There was something very strange about it, and it took Brian a moment to realize what it was. Though the drawbridge was down, the gates open and the portcullis up, there was no one about: no men-at-arms walked the parapet or stood guard at the gatehouse.

Tertius had taken out his telescope and was scanning the ramparts on top of the bailey wall, the arrow slits of the keep beyond it. He handed it to Brian, and Brian looked through it also. But even with the spyglass he could detect no movement, no sign of life anywhere.

"It's either deserted, abandoned," he said, "or it's a trap."

"It's a trap," said Maude flatly.

"Probably. Do we go in anyway?"

"If we don't, someone will be very disappointed," said Maude. "And of course we'll never know whether it was or it wasn't."

Brian glanced at Tertius.

"If we agreed before that we've come too far

to turn back," he said, "why should we do so now?"

Brian nodded and they went forward across the barren, windswept ground and then across the drawbridge. The horses' hooves echoed as they rode through the arch of the gatehouse. Then, as they reached the courtyard beyond it, the portcullis came crashing down behind them.

"That's that," said Maude. "Now we do know."

There was no one in the courtyard, no sign of who had dropped the portcullis, but the door of the great hall on the far side of the courtyard stood open. They dismounted and went toward it, pausing on the threshold while Brian drew Starflame. Then they went in.

Though the sun had not yet set, the great hall was shadowy, lit only by candles on the high table. By this dim light they could see that the hall was empty except for three people who sat at the high table: two knights and a lady. The knights, one dressed in crimson and the other in blue, were young. The lady who sat between them was ageless.

The knights, heavyset and jowly, were eating, and they continued to eat as Brian, Maude and Tertius walked the length of the hall toward them. Only the lady, toying with a goblet, watched them. She wore black: a tightly fitting black dress with white lace at the throat. Her hair was dark and glossy, her skin very white and her mouth very red. She was very beautiful and at the same time as dangerous-looking as an unsheathed dagger.

Surprisingly, it was Tertius who spoke first.

"Well," he said. "Greetings, Primus. And to you too, Secundus."

The bones they had been gnawing still in their hands, the two knights looked at him, looked again and then looked at one another.

"No," said the one in crimson. "It can't be."

"I'm afraid it is," said the one in blue.

"I admit it looks like him, but he's at Ferlay doing his service."

"Perhaps he's finished."

"Then why isn't he home? What's he doing here?"

"I don't know. Why don't you ask him?"

"All right. I will. Tertius, what are you doing here?"

"I hate to interrupt," said the dark lady, "but if the young man is a friend of yours, you might introduce him to me."

"What?" said the knight in crimson. "Oh, sorry. Only he isn't a friend. He's our brother."

"His name's Tertius," said the one in blue. "It means the Third. Primus," he nodded toward his companion, "Secundus and Tertius. First, second and third. It was Father's idea."

"A little mechanical," said the dark lady, "but quite logical. And the others?"

"Haven't the faintest idea," said Primus. "Who are they, Tertius?"

"Friends of mine," said Tertius. "This is Maude and this is Brian of Caercorbin."

"And why have you come here?" asked the dark lady.

"May I ask who you are first, madam?" asked Tertius politely.

"I don't see why not. I am the Lady Viviane, sometimes known as Nimue."

"Oh," said Tertius, looking at her with great interest. "Of course. I should have known. As to why we have come . . ." He glanced at Brian.

"We are looking for the Knight with the Red Shield, my lady," said Brian.

"I see," said Nimue. "Do we have a knight with a red shield here?" she asked Primus.

"You mean down in the dungeons?"

"Anywhere."

"Not that I know of. Do you know of any knight with a red shield? Secundus?"

"I never really look at their shields, but I don't think so."

"Nevertheless I have reason to believe that he is here, my lady," said Brian. "He is, in fact, your cousin."

"My cousin?" She stared at him. "What in heaven's name do you want with him?"

"It's a long story. Then you admit that he is here?"

"How dare you question me here in my own castle?"

"*Is* it yours?"

"Ah," she said. "That does it. Primus!"

"Yes?"

"Well, don't just sit there like a lump of lard! Take care of him!"

"You mean take him prisoner?"

"Of course."

"Somehow I don't think that's going to be so easy," he said, studying Brian. "I have a feeling he'll fight."

"Are you afraid of him?"

"Why, no. Not really. Naturally I'm prepared to do a certain amount of fighting. But I don't like the looks of that sword of his. I have a feeling that it may be magical."

"It is," said Tertius.

"There you are," said Primus. "After all, I took care of the last one. Why doesn't Secundus take care of him?"

"May I ask," said Nimue quietly, "just why the two of you are here, if you are not even willing to render me so small a service?"

"You know why," said Primus. "Bedegraine is a nice enough place, but this is even nicer; a larger fief and much richer. One of these days you'll get tired of being a maiden lady—you're not getting any younger, you know—and then you'll marry me or possibly Secundus."

"I'd rather marry a serf," she said intensely, "or a Saracen! Is it help you want?"

She gestured and suddenly the great hall was flooded with light as men-at-arms bearing torches poured in from the doorways and from behind the arrases.

"That's all very well, Nimue," said Primus sulkily, "but if it is a magic sword, someone's still going to get hurt."

"Then what do you suggest?"

"Why don't you take care of him yourself?"

She looked at him, at Secundus, then at Maude.

"This is what happens when you're a woman," she said, "especially one with responsibilities. You're alone, weak, and helpless, so you search out men—brave, wise, masterly men—who will share your burdens, help you to satisfy your simple needs. Men who will comfort and sustain you, advise you, teach and protect you. And what happens?" Her voice rose. "You end up surrounded by incompetents, fools and cowards! Knights who won't fight, an alchemist who dissolves gold instead of making it. . . ."

"Now, Nimue," began Primus.

"Be quiet! You'd like me to take care of him? Very well. Look at me," she said to Brian. "Into my eyes."

"No!" said Maude urgently. "Don't!"

Brian had been looking at Nimue, and now he tried to look away, but her dark eyes held his as a magnet holds steel.

"Have you ever heard the tale of Caradoc," she said conversationally, "who was known as Brise Bras, He of the Wasted Arm? It's a fascinating story. He angered an enchanter whose familiar was a serpent—a serpent like this one."

As she spoke, she slipped a gold bracelet off her arm: a bracelet cunningly wrought in the shape of a coiling serpent.

"The enchanter sent the serpent, which was of course invisible, to Caradoc as I send this one to you." She tossed the bracelet across the table so that it fell at Brian's feet. "Seeing its prey, the serpent leaped up, coiled around Caradoc's arm, as mine is coiling round yours, and gripped it so tightly that Caradoc's arm became paralyzed, powerless, dead."

"Don't look at her! Don't listen to her!" said Maude.

But it was too late. His eyes on Nimue's, unable to tear them away, Brian saw the gold serpent writhing toward him. Suddenly his right arm was seized, gripped by some constricting force. He tried to raise it, free it, but it was becoming numb, weak. The numbness spread downward until it reached his hand, then, as he stared incredulously, Starflame slipped from his nerveless fingers and clattered to the stone floor.

"Yes," said Nimue. "Like that. All right, Primus."

Rising, Primus came around the high table toward Brian. But when he bent down to pick up Starflame, Tertius spoke.

"I wouldn't touch it if I were you."

"Why not?" asked Primus.

"Go ahead, then. You'll see."

As Primus hesitated, glancing at Nimue, Tertius picked up the sword himself and slipped it back into the sheath that hung at Brian's side. Without thinking, Brian gripped it with his left hand, holding it firmly.

"It doesn't matter," said Nimue to Primus. "He can't use it. Take him. Take all of them away."

CHAPTER SIXTEEN

PLEASE," SAID MAUDE.

Slowly Brian raised his eyes. She was still kneeling in front of him, holding out a piece of the bread the guard had brought in early that morning. He shook his head.

"I'm not hungry," he said.

"I know. You said that. But you've got to eat."

"To keep up my strength?"

"Yes." Then, as he continued to sit there, huddled in the corner of the cell, "Stop looking at me that way!" she said sharply." And stop feeling so sorry for yourself!"

He blinked at her intensity.

"Is that what I've been doing?"

"You know it is! You've been sitting there like a lost gazehound ever since they brought us down here. And I'm getting sick of it! Have you lost your arm?"

It was resting limply on his lap, and he glanced down at it.

"No," he explained patiently. "But you see, I can't use it. . . ."

For some reason this made her angrier than ever.

"Don't you think we know that? But we told you there must be something that can be done about that, some way of lifting the spell she put on you. And if there is, we'll find it. But you've got to help us."

"By eating?"

"To begin with, yes!"

He sighed, wishing there was some way he could make her understand without having to talk about it. For talking, even thinking, took a great effort. He seemed to remember a time—could it only have been yesterday?—when what had happened had meant a great deal to him. What she didn't seem to realize, and what he hadn't the strength to tell her, was that now it wasn't just his arm that was numb. It was as if the numbness had spread so that now not only did nothing mean anything to him, but he didn't *feel* anything: not anger or affection, not sorrow or fear—nothing.

He had been looking at her, into her eyes, and now he saw that instead of the impatience he had heard in her voice there was concern in them, deep concern. And somehow that touched him as no words could have done.

"All right," he said.

Taking the bread from her, he bit into it. It was stale, hard.

"Not very good, is it?" she said.

He shook his head.

"Still, it's food. Would you like some water?"

He nodded, and she held up the jug that the guard had brought in with the bread. He drank and, with an effort, swallowed the bread.

"Now let me look at your arm again." Putting down the jug, she began kneading his shoulder muscle. "Do you feel that?"

"Yes."

"What about this?" Still kneading, massaging, she slid her hand further down his arm. He shook his head.

"You don't feel anything here?"

"No. It's no use, Maude. It seems to me that you tried this before."

"And I'll keep on trying. It can't do any harm. And if I could get someone else to help me . . ." She glared at Tertius who was still at the door of the cell, looking out through the small grilled opening.

He turned.

"What did you say?"

"I said, if I could get someone else to help me with this—meaning you—"

"Oh. Of course. But you know, that *is* a laboratory at the end of the corridor. The guard just came out, and I could see into it."

"What of it?"

"I told you, I don't mind helping you massage his arm. But I think a far better thing would be to get out of here."

"Out of this dungeon?"

"Away from here altogether."

"And you think you can arrange that?" asked Maude ironically.

"Yes. I'm sorry it took me so long to figure out how to do it, but . . ." Turning back to the door, he called, "Guard! Ho there, Guard!"

After he had shouted and rattled the door a few times, the guard appeared; a long-nosed, swarthy man with a scar on his cheek.

"What do you want?" he growled.

"I want to talk to the Lady Nimue."

"You want to . . . ?"

"Yes. And if you know what's good for you, you'll get her."

The guard stared at him, started to guffaw. Then, as Tertius returned his look calmly and coolly, he changed his mind. He stood there uncertainly for a moment. Then, muttering to himself, he went away.

"She won't come," said Maude. "Why should she?"

"Because she's a woman."

"What does that mean?"

"She'll be curious as to what I want to talk to her about."

A short while later there were footsteps in the corridor outside, and Nimue's face appeared in the barred opening of the heavy door.

"I understand you wanted to talk to me," she said.

"Yes," said Tertius. "I apologize for disturbing you, but unfortunately I couldn't come to *you.*"

"At least he has a sense of humor," she said to Primus and Secundus who stood behind her. "Which is more than I can say for some of his relatives." Then to Tertius, "I assume it was about something important."

"Let's say about something I think you'll find interesting. But talking this way," he gestured toward the grilled opening, "is rather awkward."

She studied him for a moment, then ordered, "Open the door." When the guard had done so, she demanded, "Well?"

"About a quarter of a mile from here," said Tertius, pointing to the cell's barred window, "is an island. There's a cliff on this side of it. And on a ledge about halfway up the cliff is a gull's nest. How many eggs are there in it?"

"Is this a riddle?" she asked.

"No."

"Then I don't know. I've never been there."

"Neither have I. But there are three eggs in it."

"How do you know?"

Taking his telescope from his belt, he extended it to its full length and handed it to her. She looked at it curiously, then walking to the window of the cell, put it to her eye and looked through it. She started as the image came into focus, but when she lowered the telescope, her face was expressionless.

"Yes, there are three eggs in it. What of it?"

Taking the telescope from her, he reversed it. Then, pointing to the doorway of the cell where Primus and Secundus stood with the guard, "My dear brothers are very close to us, are they not? So close that you can almost reach out and touch them." And when she nodded, "Look at them through this."

Putting the large end of the telescope to her eye, she looked toward the cell door. Again she started, and her hand went out as if to make sure that what she saw was as far away as it seemed. But again, when she lowered the telescope, her face was expressionless.

"An interesting toy," she said, handing it back to him. "I'm sure you had some purpose in showing it to me."

"Of course. It is, as you say, an interesting toy, and I showed it to you, not to impress you, but in the way of an analogy. I know something about your powers, knew about them before we ever came here. But I wondered if it had ever occurred to you that if it is possible to master distance—bring the far near and make the near seem far—it is possible to do the same thing with time. That it is possible, in fact, to reverse it."

"Reverse it?"

"I thought you might be interested because of something Primus said yesterday, something rather ungallant."

"That I was not getting any younger?" She laughed, but her laugh was harsh. "Who is?"

"I know of one person who is." And he glanced at Maude.

"She?" Nimue looked at her too. "You'll have to do better than that if you want to impress me. She's old enough to be my mother."

"She is. But when Brian and I first met her she was old enough to be your grandmother—or your great-grandmother."

Again Nimue looked at Maude, then at Tertius.

"You're not at all like your brothers," she said. "You're a very clever young man, and I'm not sure I can trust you. But your friend here is something else again." She turned to Brian who was still sitting in the corner of the cell. "Look at me!" she said. Then, when her eyes were holding his as they had the day before in the great hall, she asked, "Is what he says true?"

Brian nodded.

"She is getting younger?"

He nodded again.

"You would not lie," she said thoughtfully. "In fact, you could not—not to me. And I have heard of such a thing. You, Tertius, you know how it's done?"

"I think so. And of course I'll have her to help me. But since the process involved is alchemical and rather complicated, we'll need a laboratory to work in."

"I can provide that. And an old dotard who

calls himself an alchemist along with it. But you haven't told me what you want in exchange for this miraculous elixir or potion or whatever it may be."

"First of all, our freedom. And in addition . . . shall we say as much gold as we can carry away with us?"

She considered this. "That sounds fair enough. After all, what have I to lose?" Then, to Primus and Secundus, she added, "take the two of them into the laboratory."

"The three of us," said Maude.

"All right. The three of them. And tell Alwyn that he, as well as the laboratory, is to be at their disposal. How long will it take?"

"It's hard to say," said Tertius. "It depends on many things. But we should have something for you, at least a progress report, in a day or so."

"Very well."

She stepped back and stood watching as Primus, Secundus, and the guard led them along the passageway.

"So you've become a magician," said Primus to Tertius as they stopped in front of a heavy oaken door.

"It's something I've always wanted to be," said Tertius. "Does that surprise you?"

"Nothing you could say or do would surprise me," said Primus.

"I wonder," said Tertius.

"I'm not sure I like this," grumbled Secundus. "I mean, if he has learned any magic . . ."

"If he knew as much as Nimue, would they be here now?" asked Primus.

"No. I suppose not."

The guard had been fumbling with his keys. Finally finding the one he wanted, he unlocked the door and they went in, followed by Primus and Secundus.

They found themselves in a large, square, stone-walled room with barred windows on three sides of it. A furnace glowed in one corner, and on the coals, in a bain-marie, was a huge alembic with a greenish liquid bubbling in it. There were jars, bottles, and flasks on the shelves and on the long wooden table in the center of the room. Scattered here and there, on the table and on the floor, were retorts, hourglasses, mortars and pestles, crucibles and astrolabes.

The room was silent except for a strange whistling sound, and at first it seemed empty.

"Alwyn!" called Primus.

The whistling sound turned into a snort, and a man's face appeared above the table edge. It was round, pink-cheeked and not merely bald, but completely hairless, without either eyebrows or eyelashes.

"What?" he said, blinking large, blue, innocent eyes at them. "Oh, it's you, Primus. I was so deep in thought I didn't hear you come in."

"Thought?" said Primus. "You were asleep!"

"Was I? Perhaps I was. I was up all night, working on a new formula. Tell Nimue that I am close, very close. After the filtration, calcination, probation and rubification . . ."

"Never mind that," said Primus. "She said you're to stop whatever you're doing and help him," he jerked his head toward Tertius, "with what he's going to do."

"Oh?" said Alwyn. "Of course. Delighted. But just the same, I think she should know . . ."

"We'll tell her," said Secundus. "Come on, Primus. The air in here's foul, and besides, I'm hungry."

"When aren't you?" asked Primus. "As for you," he said to Tertius, "you'd better have what you promised her very soon. She's had it up to here with people who talk big and don't deliver." And with a baleful glance at Alwyn, he and Secundus left the laboratory.

"I can't imagine what he's talking about," said Alwyn as the guard closed and locked the door. "Can you?"

"No," said Tertius.

"If she's complaining about me . . . Forgive me, I'm afraid I don't know your name."

"Tertius. And Maude and Brian."

"How do you do?" said the man, coming around from behind the table. He was short, not much taller than Tertius, and quite plump. "I'm Alwyn, and . . . Tertius? That's a strange coincidence. Those two hulking brutes who were just in here are Primus and Secundus."

"I know," said Tertius. "They're my brothers."

"Oh? I'm sorry."

"So am I," said Tertius.

"Am I to take it, then, that you don't find them—shall we say—congenial?"

"That," said Tertius, "is putting it very mildly."

"I'm delighted to hear it. And all the more delighted to meet you," he said, shaking Tertius's hand enthusiastically. "And you, madam. And you, sir." Then, "Is there something wrong with your arm?" he asked Brian.

"She put a spell on it," said Tertius. "He can't use it."

"That's bad," said Alwyn, suddenly serious. "She casts a very powerful spell. I'm afraid I can't do anything to counter it; magic's not my field. But I have some very good liniment here."

"I don't think that will help," said Maude. "Tertius thinks that the best thing we can do is to get away from here."

"An excellent idea," said Alwyn. "Find some friendly enchanter who can lift the spell. I've often thought of it myself—getting away, I mean. But it won't be easy. As you saw, they keep the door locked."

"I know," said Tertius. "But I still think I can manage."

"Well, if I can assist you in any way . . . She said I should, didn't she?"

"Yes," said Tertius. "It might save time if I told you what I needed and you got it for me. First of all, sulphur."

"Of course. What kind?"

"Is there more than one kind?"

"Oh, yes. There are many kinds. The red

and the white sulphurs of Marcasita, the yellow and black sulphurs of Talc, the purple and black sulphurs of Cachimiae, the red sulphur of cinnabar . . ."

"Yellow sulphur."

"Are you sure? It's the commonest kind."

"I'm sure."

"Very well," said Alwyn, taking down a large earthenware crock. "What else?"

"Potassium nitrate."

"Potassium? I'm afraid I don't know that. Is it a liquid or a solid? An earth, a metal, a chalk, a salt . . ."

"A salt. Also known as niter or saltpeter."

"Ah, sal petrae. I have that. What else?"

"Charcoal."

"Is there anything I can do in the meantime?" asked Maude.

"As a matter of fact, there is," said Tertius. "Let me see." He walked around the laboratory, looking at the walls, the floor. "Here," he said, pointing to the corner nearest the door. "Do you have any tools?" he asked Alwyn.

"What sort?"

"A hammer and chisel or a pick."

"Unfortunately, no," said Alwyn.

"Never mind. This will do," said Tertius, picking up the poker that leaned against the furnace and giving it to Maude. "Start digging there, in that corner."

"In case you hadn't noticed," said Maude, "there's a huge rock just outside. And if that's the way you intend to get out, by digging . . ."

"It's not," said Tertius. "But we're going to need a hole: not a large one, but a fairly deep one."

"All right. Come on, Brian."

Taking him by the arm, she led him to the corner of the laboratory and sat him down on a stool. Then, studying the place Tertius had indicated, she drove the point of the poker into a crack between the floor and the wall. Feeling like a child who has been told to sit quietly and not bother anyone, Brian watched her. Behind him he could hear Tertius and the strange, hairless man talking as they poured things from crocks and jars, weighing, mixing and measuring them. Finally, when Maude paused for a moment to rest, he rose. "Let me," he said.

"You?" She looked at him. "Can you?"

"I don't know. But let me try."

Taking the poker from her, he knelt down beside the hole she had started and began chipping away at the mortar as she had been doing. It was difficult, working with only one hand, and his left hand at that, and soon he was breathing hard and bathed with perspiration. But he kept at it until his left arm felt almost as numb as his right.

"I'm sorry," he said.

"That's enough," said Maude gruffly. "Give it to me." And taking the poker from him, she bent over the hole again. As she did, it seemed to Brian that her eyes were not merely soft, but misty.

They worked at the hole, taking turns, for some time. At first it went slowly but, when they were through the mortar and had reached the rubble underneath, it went more quickly. Finally, when the hole was almost two feet deep, Tertius came over to look at it and said, "I think that will do."

He motioned to Alwyn, who brought him a large basin filled with coarse black powder. He poured the powder into the hole, ramming it down with the poker. Then, picking up the basin, he walked backward, pouring carefully as he went, so that he made a fine trail of the remaining powder, which reached almost to the furnace.

"I have been practicing the spagyric arts for more than twenty years," said Alwyn. "I have read the *Summa Perfectionis,* know the Seven Canons of the Metals and have myself assisted at the birth of the Red Lion. But I must confess that I do not understand what you are about."

"There's no reason why you should," said Tertius, putting down the basin.

"But if alchemy is an art, and it is, then it

must follow certain laws and rules."

"It does," said Tertius. "Help me clear off the table.

"Clear it off?"

"Yes."

While Alwyn was protesting, Maude came over; and she and Tertius removed the bottles, flasks and jars from the long heavy table.

"Now what?" she asked.

"Help me move it over there."

Together they dragged it to the corner farthest from the one where they had made the hole, then Tertius tipped it over so that it fell on its side with a crash.

"Why did you do *that*?" wailed Alwyn.

"You'll see," said Tertius, pushing it back until it was diagonally in front of the corner, making a kind of barricade. "Get behind there, all of you, and lie down flat, as flat as you can."

"But won't you at least explain . . . ?" begged Alwyn as they did so.

"Of course," said Tertius, crouching down

behind the table with them. "There's nothing to be afraid of. I hope," he added under his breath. "Was it not Al Gebir who said, 'Fire is the beginning and the end, summing up in itself all things'?"

"Yes," said Alwyn.

"Then let us add fire to what we already have." And taking the tongs from beside the furnace, he picked up a glowing coal and dropped it on the end of the trail of black powder.

The stone floor of the laboratory was uneven, higher in some places than in others. And lying between Maude and Alwyn, Brian found he could look under the bottom edge of the table and see what occurred next.

For a moment, nothing happened. Then, as if it had been stung to life, the black powder sparked and crackled, and fire sped along its length to the far corner. As Brian drew back, shutting his eyes, there was a deafening, earsplitting roar, louder than a thunderclap, and he felt the floor under him heave and shudder as if the whole castle were being shaken like a dicebox.

Brian continued to lie there, eyes still closed, in the silence that followed.

"Who did that?" demanded a furious voice.

Opening his eyes, Brian raised his head cautiously and looked over the top of the table. The whole of the far corner of the laboratory was gone, leaving a gaping opening. The huge rock just outside the laboratory wall was gone too, shattered into a hundred pieces. And standing on a pile of rubble and framed by what remained of the wall, was a strange but commanding figure: an elderly man with a white beard. He wore a long, dark robe, and on his head was a small round cap embroidered with cabalistic signs. Silhouetted against the sky, he glared at the four heads that showed above the upper edge of the overturned table. And dazed and shaken though Brian was, when the old man's eyes bored into his, he knew who he was, who he must be.

CHAPTER SEVENTEEN

"I SAID, WHO DID that?" repeated the white-bearded man.

Slowly, Tertius stood up.

"I'm afraid I did," he said.

The elderly man's eyes, blue and cold as a winter sky, swung to him.

"And do you know *what* you did?" he asked.

"I think so," said Tertius.

"You think!" said the elderly man severely. "You flout history—the logical development of science—are responsible for an outrageous anachronism, and you *think* . . . Who are you?"

"Tertius."

"That's not a name, it's a number. Unless . . ." He came down off the pile of rubble and into the laboratory. "Tertius of Bedegraine?"

"Yes," said Tertius. "And you . . . are you Merlin?"

"Of course," said the elderly man testily. "Who else would I be? But that still doesn't explain how you did it. I know I endowed you with knowledge, a great deal of knowledge, but . . ." He paused. "Oh, no!"

"Yes," said Tertius. "I'm not being critical because, while it's been awkward, it's also been very interesting. But I'm afraid the knowledge you gave me was all *future* knowledge, and . . ."

"Say no more," said Merlin. "I know what happened now. And how it happened. The question is what the results will be. That was gunpowder you used, wasn't it?"

"Yes."

"And do you know when it is first supposed to be used here?"

"Yes," said Tertius. "Of course the Chinese have known about it for some time now."

"Just a second," said Merlin. He stood there for

a moment as if listening. "Apparently it's all right. But don't do it again. Or anything like it. Now what's going on here? Who are these people?"

"This is Maude and this is Brian of Caercorbin," said Tertius. "They're my friends and companions. And this is Alwyn. He's an alchemist."

"Oh, yes," said Merlin, looking at Alwyn. "She would get herself an alchemist. Had you working on the transformation of lead to gold, I suppose?"

"Yes, master," said Alwyn. "But of course that's not what I'm really interested in."

"Naturally," said Merlin. "What you're interested in is something just as fantastic and ridiculous: the Lapis Philosophorum."

"Ridiculous?" said Alwyn.

"Yes," said Merlin. "I don't like interfering in a man's career, but I don't like to see him wasting his time either. The Philosopher's Stone doesn't exist and never will. What's wrong with your arm?" he asked Brian.

"The Lady Nimue put a spell on it," said Brian.

"Oh?" He turned to Tertius. "Which spell was it?"

"I don't know," said Tertius. "What it's called, I mean. That's one of the things I want to learn—how to do magic, use what I know in an appropriate way. But . . ."

"She set a serpent, an invisible serpent, on him," said Maude. "It's still coiled around his arm."

"The Caradoc bit," said Merlin, nodding. "She always had a weakness for Welsh magic. Well, we'll soon take care of that." He raised his hand, then paused. "No. I've got a few other bones to pick with her. I think we'll make her lift it herself. Come on." And he started for the door.

"Were you planning to go upstairs?" asked Tertius.

"Of course. Why?"

"In the first place, the door's locked. That's why I blasted a hole in the wall. But, apart from that, do you think it's wise? I mean, wasn't it

Nimue who put a spell on you, imprisoned you under a rock?"

"In other words, you think that she knows more than I do."

"I wouldn't go that far," said Tertius, hesitantly.

"I can see that, for many reasons, it's a good thing I came back," said Merlin. "As for the door . . ." Turning toward it, he pursed his lips and puffed gently, as if he were blowing the seeds off a dandelion. Immediately the door began shaking, rattling, then—as if struck by a hurricane blast—it burst open, splitting from top to bottom.

"Mind the splinters," said Merlin, leading the way through.

They followed him along the corridor, which had small, dark cells on both sides of it. Gaunt faces peered out at them through the grilled openings in the doors.

"Excuse me," said Brian, pausing in front of one of them. "But don't you think we might . . . ?"

"Yes, but not now," said Merlin, beginning

to climb the narrow, spiral stairs. "I'm much too anxious to see my dear pupil."

Nimue was in the great hall when they entered it. She was sitting at the high table between Primus and Secundus with a dozen or more men-at-arms ranged along the wall behind her.

"So it *was* you," she said to Merlin. "We wondered what that noise was."

"Why didn't you send to find out?" he asked.

"Because I'm surrounded by lily-livered poltroons. They were afraid to go. Was that really necessary, Merlin? The whole castle shook till we thought it would come down about our ears."

"As it happens, it wasn't I who did it. It was my young friend here," and he nodded toward Tertius.

"Ah," she said. "I knew he was clever, but I still seem to have underestimated him. Well, we'll soon remedy that."

She started to raise her hand.

"I wouldn't if I were you, Nimue," said Merlin.

"What did you say?"

"I said I wouldn't if I were you."

"Are you threatening me?"

"I rarely threaten," he said. "As you should know. I'd far rather advise."

"Well, let me give *you* some advice, you old dotard!" she said with sudden venom. "I don't know how you got out from under that rock. But if you interfere in my affairs, I'll put you back under it again."

"Just a second," said Merlin. "What was that you called me? A dotard?"

"Yes!" she said furiously. "A stupid and ridiculous, doddering, senile . . ."

"Spare me the adjectives," said Merlin, still quietly. "I take your meaning. Now let me clear up a few things. Do you really believe I didn't know what you had in mind when you showed me that chamber under the rock?"

"Then why did you go in? You were there for more than ten years."

"Was it as long as that? It seemed like only a few days—quiet, peaceful days. And the truth is, my dear Nimue, that after listening to your incessant chatter, peace and quiet was what I wanted more than anything else. Do you understand what I'm trying to tell you? I was bored, bored, bored to death with you. That's why I went in there. And that's why I stayed there—to get away from you. But now . . . thunder and lightning!" he shouted suddenly. Lightning flashed and crackled overhead, and thunder rumbled and roared. "Fire and brimstone!" Flames leaped up from the stone floor, and the air became thick and heavy with the smell of burning sulphur. "Do you think that you or anyone else could keep me prisoner against my will?" His eyes blazed, blue sparks crackled in a nimbus around his head and his white beard stood out stiff and straight, like an accusing finger. "You have a smattering of grammarie, know the few spells I taught you, but do you dare compare your knowledge to mine? You can call up a storm or quiet one, but can you do this?"

He raised his hand and, as the thunder continued rumbling, the lightning flashing and the flames burning, it began raining in one corner of the great hall, snowing in another, hailing in the third while, in the last, a whirlwind spun and danced, whipping pitchers, goblets and even benches up to the rooftree.

The men-at-arms were groveling on the floor; Primus and Secundus had slid under the table; and only Nimue remained where she was. But her face was paler than ever.

Again Merlin raised his hand and the thunder ceased, the flames died and it stopped blowing, snowing, raining and hailing.

"Enough, my dear Nimue?" asked Merlin in the sudden silence that followed.

She nodded.

"Good. Don't provoke me again or I'll forget our past relationship and turn you into something thoroughly unpleasant, say, a wart on the belly of the biggest frog in the fens of Reith."

She shuddered, and he went on. "Now there are a few more things we had better talk about. First of all, the little plot you've been working on so diligently."

"The plot?"

He looked at her witheringly. "Even if I didn't know you, don't you think I'd guess what you were up to; enticing knights here, trying to buy their allegiance, and locking up those you couldn't buy in your dungeons? There will be no march on Camelot. Is that understood?"

Once more she nodded.

"Good again. Next we have the matter of the spell you put on this young man, the friend of my godson, Tertius."

"If you don't mind, Merlin," said Tertius unexpectedly, "I've been thinking about it and, now that I have you standing by, I'd like to take care of that."

"Oh?" Merlin looked at him searchingly. "Why not? Go ahead."

"Nimue never finished the story of

Caradoc," said Tertius to Brian. "She never told you how he was freed of the invisible serpent. Because it is possible to get rid of it."

"How?" asked Brian.

"It calls for a good deal of courage and self-sacrifice," said Tertius, "not on your part but on that of someone else. For the spell can be transferred. If there is anyone who cares enough for you to become the victim in your stead, the serpent can be forced to leave your arm and go to that other person."

"Then we'd better forget about it," said Brian. "Because I'd never permit that. And even if I would, where could she find such a person?"

"That's not too difficult," said Maude. "I'll do it."

"You?" Brian looked at her in astonishment. "Why should you?"

"That's my business," said Maude harshly. "Go on."

"No!" said Brian. "I said I'd never permit

it, and I certainly wouldn't let you, of all people . . ."

"Be quiet!" said Merlin.

"I won't!" said Brian. "I tell you I won't have it!"

"Silence him," said Merlin, apparently to the empty air. "And hold him."

Before Brian could move, what seemed to be an invisible hand was clapped to his mouth, making it impossible for him to speak, while other hands gripped and held him.

"All right, Tertius," said Merlin.

"I think I should explain," said Tertius to Maude, "that I cannot be certain what the serpent will do when it leaves Brian's arm. It might coil about your neck instead of your arm. . . ."

"It doesn't matter," said Maude, and though she was now as pale as Nimue had been, her voice was steady. "Go ahead."

"Very well," said Tertius. "Stand here." And he placed her to Brian's right, two or three feet away from him. Taking his spectacles from his pouch, he put them on and peered at Brian's arm. Then, as Brian strained at the unseen hands that were holding him, Tertius hissed softly and said, *"Serpens invisus, serpens saevus, audite!* Listen, listen well and obey. By Azoc, Zoar, Amioram, Methon and Tafrac, *iubeo ire!* Go!"

"Well?" asked Merlin.

"It's starting to move, loosen its coils," said Tertius, still peering through his spectacles, watching intently. And as he spoke, Brian felt a tingling, a prickling in the arm that had been numb for so long. Suddenly Tertius moved, and moved with surprising speed. Reaching out, he whipped Starflame from the sheath at Brian's side and slashed down savagely between him and Maude. There was a faint tinkling sound as of glass breaking.

"Did you get him?" asked Merlin.

"See for yourself," said Tertius, pointing with the sword.

Looking down, Brian saw a small pool of silvery droplets on the floor near his feet.

"It must have been a Cornish, not a Welsh serpent," said Merlin. "They're the only ones that have mercury for blood. Well done, Tertius. You have talent, definite talent."

"Thank you," said Tertius. Reversing Starflame, he held it out. "Here, Brian."

Without thinking, Brian took the sword from him. And it was only after he had done so that he realized he had taken it with his right hand.

"I can use it!" he said. "I can use my arm again!"

"Of course," said Tertius.

"And you're all right?" Brian asked Maude.

Taking a deep breath, Maude nodded.

"It never touched her," explained Tertius. "I killed it as Cador did the serpent that was coiled round Caradoc's arm in midair, when it was leaving you for her."

Sheathing Starflame, Brian clasped Tertius's hand, then turned to Maude.

"What can I say to you?" he asked quietly. "How am I to thank you for what you did?"

"There's nothing to thank me for," she said. "For I did nothing."

"Nothing?"

"No. But if you must say something, you can say to me what I said to you when you saved me from the boar. You can tell me I'm a fool." Then, as he continued looking at her, she said, "Can't we get on with what brought us here? Have you forgotten who is down there in the dungeons?"

"No," said Brian. "I haven't forgotten. I hate to trouble you," he said to Merlin, "but when we were coming up here you said we might free the prisoners."

"That's right," said Merlin. "The prisoners. Was there any special one you were interested in?"

"Yes. Her cousin, the Knight with the Red Shield."

"Her cousin? I didn't know she had one." He turned to Nimue. "Release him. Release all of them, give them their arms and have them brought up here."

CHAPTER EIGHTEEN

"WILL YOU PLEASE stop that?" said Maude, pulling her hood forward.

"Stop what?"

"Staring at me like that."

"I'm sorry," said Brian. He glanced at Nimue who was sitting quietly but sulkily at the high table, and then at Merlin and Tertius who were standing nearby, deep in conversation. "What do you suppose they're talking about?"

"What do you think?"

"Magic. Tertius was looking for a teacher and he's found one, the greatest one of all."

"Yes, his quest seems to be over. And so does yours."

With a curious pang, Brian realized that this was true.

"I suppose it is."

"You don't sound very happy about it."

"But I am. What's the point of a quest if you don't find what you're looking for? It's just . . . what about yours?"

"What about it?"

"I don't even know what it is. You've never told us."

"And never will."

"All right. But why can't I help you with it?"

"Are you that anxious to continue questing? I would have thought you'd want to return to Meliot."

"Well, yes. I suppose I'll have to do that, go there with the Knight with the Red Shield. Tertius said our three quests were intertwined and so far he's been right. Perhaps he'll come with us."

"I think he will. At least as far as Meliot."

"You mean you're going back there too?"

"Why not? That's where our quests began—yours and mine—and that's where they'll end: yours with your princess, the beautiful Alys."

"Don't, Maude. Please," he said awkwardly.

"Why? Isn't that why you undertook your quest?"

"Yes, it is. But . . ."

There was a tramp of boots, a shuffling of feet behind them, and they turned to watch as the prisoners, with an escort of men-at-arms, came into the great hall. There were about a dozen of them. A few of them were thin, emaciated, their clothes ragged, but all of them bore their arms and walked proudly. Their leader was a tall knight who looked strangely familiar, and as he drew near and Brian saw his straw-colored hair and long mustachios . . .

"Sir Uriel!" he said.

"What?" The tall knight peered at him. "Well, hello. I remember you. We met at

Meliot. You're the squire who fought the Black Knight. What are you doing here?" He jerked his head at Nimue. "She take you prisoner, too?"

"Yes," said Brian. "For a while."

"Nasty business. She always was a sly minx. Took up with Merlin some years ago." He paused, his eyes on the elderly enchanter. "Excuse me, but aren't you . . . ?"

"Yes," said Merlin.

"I thought so. Saw you once at Camelot when I was a page. May I ask whose side you're on here?"

"Not hers," said Merlin.

"Oh. That's good. Then we should be able to handle her. And it's time someone did. Because, do you know what she's been up to, this dear cousin of mine?"

"Cousin?" said Brian. "Is Nimue your cousin?"

"Yes, of course. That's why I came here."

"But then—you must be the Knight with the Red Shield!"

"What?" Sir Uriel swung his shield forward and looked down at it. "Not that I know of. How can I be?"

Brian, Maude and Tertius looked at the shield also. It was somewhat battered, but it wasn't red. It was green as midsummer grass.

"I don't understand," said Brian. "Giles the Giant said it was red."

"Did you meet him?" asked Tertius.

"The giant?" said Sir Uriel. "Yes, of course. Fine fellow. Gave me some ale in the biggest drinking horn I've ever seen."

"The dragon's horn," said Brian. "And he claimed that the only other person who'd drunk from it recently was a knight with a red shield."

"Achromatopsia," said Tertius. "Also called daltonism. I should have guessed." Then, as they all stared at him, "Giles is color-blind, can't tell the difference between green and red."

"Now that you mention it," said Maude, "his sister wasn't sure that the shield was red."

"Then we've been on a false trail, a

wild-goose chase, ever since we left there," said Brian unhappily. "What are we going to do now? The dragon's horn was the only clue we had. Can't you help us, sir?" he asked Merlin. "It was you who said that the only knight in the world who could overthrow the Black Knight and save Meliot was the Knight with the Red Shield."

"Did I?" said Merlin. "Then it must be true."

"Won't you help us, then? Tell us where we can find him?"

"I suppose I could," said Merlin.

"Wait," said Tertius. He and Maude had been looking at one another, both with strange expressions on their faces. And when she nodded slowly, he asked, "Will *you* help us, Sir Uriel? Will you grant us a boon?"

"Why, yes," said Sir Uriel. "If I can. But magic's not exactly my line. Or finding things or people either."

"It's nothing like that," said Tertius. "You were in Meliot when Brian challenged the Black Knight."

"Yes, I was. Good show."

"Since then he has done many brave deeds. He fought Rufus of Reith, the notorious outlaw, and rescued a woman and child Rufus had captured. He saved Maude here from a wild boar at the risk of his own life. It is he who led us to this castle and therefore it is principally because of him that you and all these other knights are free now. In the light of all this, do you not think he has earned his belt and spurs?"

"Became a knight, you mean? I should think so. I don't know if I can do anything about it right now. There's the vigil and all that. On the other hand, I suppose you could call this a field of battle. Is there anyone else who witnessed these deeds or can vouch for him?"

"I witnessed them," said Maude.

"And I'll vouch for him," said Merlin.

"That should do it," said Sir Uriel, drawing his sword. "Kneel, Brian."

"But . . ." said Brian.

Merlin crooked a finger and, as before,

unseen hands took hold of Brian and pressed him to his knees.

"With this sword," said Sir Uriel, raising it high, "which has never been drawn unjustly, in God's name and by virtue of my own knighthood, I dub thee knight." And he brought the blade down smartly on Brian's shoulder. "Rise, Sir Brian."

Slowly Brian rose to his feet.

"Thank you, Sir Uriel," he said. "I will do my utmost to be worthy of the honor you have bestowed upon me. But I still don't see why this was needed."

"Do you remember what the White Lady said to us?" asked Tertius.

"About how we'd know the Knight with the Red Shield? Of course."

"Tell us."

"She said we would know him by his sword," said Brian. "For it was forged of steel that is not of this earth." He hesitated, looking down at Starflame. "We would know him by his look. For he would have drunk from the dragon's horn and known pity as well as fear. We would know him by his strength. For he would first have lost it and then regained it. And finally, we would know him because he does not know himself." Again he paused. "You mean . . . ?"

"Yes," said Maude. "We didn't realize it either until a few minutes ago, but, now do you understand? You are the Knight with the Red Shield!"

CHAPTER NINETEEN

THE WIND HAD shifted to the northeast and, pulling his cloak more closely around him, Benedict moved around to the sheltered side of one of the towers that flanked the gate. From there, high on the battlements he could look out on the two roads that led to Meliot—the one that led to the river and the one that climbed the hill—and he could also look down on the sleeping town. For as far as he could see by the dim glow of the new moon, the roads were empty. But a few lights still showed in the palace and elsewhere in Meliot: in one or two houses and at the baker's, who had begun work earlier than usual in preparation for tomorrow. As to who would buy his special cakes and pasties, he thought grimly, that was something else again. For there was less silver in Meliot this Yule than ever before, and far less reason for celebration.

There were footsteps on the tower stairs and Gilbert, who shared the night watch with him, stepped out onto the ramparts.

"What cheer, Benedict?" he said.

"What cheer indeed?" said Benedict. "It's cold as a witch's fingers, and you're late!"

"There's nothing we can do about the cold. As for being late, Edmund just came from the palace and I waited to hear what word he brought."

"And?"

"Not good," said Gilbert. "The merchants are still closeted with the king. But so far, it seems, they are refusing to put up their share of the gold for the tribute."

"Who can blame them after all these years? Paying it has been like pouring water into a bottomless hole. What says the king?"

"He says nothing. The treasury is empty so he cannot pay it himself. There are those who think that this time he will let the Black Knight take his head."

"I had heard that also. And it might be true."

"But it can't be! What would happen to all of us?"

"What's happening to us now? How much difference is there between dying slowly, year by year, and dying quickly at one stroke?"

"A big difference," said Gilbert uneasily. "For while the king lives and Meliot endures, there is still hope."

"How much hope? Has a single champion appeared this time to take up the challenge?"

"No. At least, not yet. But . . ." He turned toward the parapet, listening. "Hark!"

Under the whistling of the wind, Benedict heard it too: the plod of horses' hooves and the clink of metal. Crossing to the parapet, he looked out through one of the crenels. Three figures were riding slowly down the hill and along the road that led to the gate. They were wrapped in worn and shabby traveling cloaks, their hoods pulled forward against the chill bite of the wind. And, as they came closer, Benedict again heard the clink of metal, which meant that at least one of them was armed.

They drew rein just under him, and the tallest of the three threw back his hood and called, "Ho there, guard! Open the gate!"

"Too late," said Benedict. "We close it at sunset. None may enter after that."

The man below him looked up, searching for him against the night sky.

"But we need food and shelter, for our beasts as well as ourselves. What are we to do?"

"Try one of the farms near the river and come back tomorrow."

Now a second of the figures looked up.

"Is that you, Benedict?"

"What?" It was a woman's voice with a note of command in it. "Why, yes. Who's that?"

"The worse for you if you don't know. And still worse if you don't open the gate! For if you don't, and at once, I'll have you whipped from here to the square!"

Mouth open, he continued to peer down into the darkness. Then, hurrying to the tower stairs, he shouted, "Ho there, below. Open the gate! And hurry!"

Gaillard pawed the ground impatiently, and Brian stroked his neck to quiet him. Then, as they heard voices, the rasp of the beams that barred the huge, ironbound doors,

"They're opening it," said Tertius.

"I thought they would," said Maude. She began edging Gracielle away from them.

"Wait, Maude," said Brian.

"For what?"

"I know you're going, but before you do there is something I would say to you."

"Well?"

"That day at Nimue's castle you asked me to repeat what the White Lady had said to me, and I did. All but the last part. Do you remember how that went?" He waited, but she said nothing. "Very well. I'll tell you. 'Accepting himself, he shall find that which he did not seek nor ever hoped to find.'"

"Well?" said Maude again.

"She was right," said Brian simply. "And since you have given me so much, there is something I would give you."

Pulling off his ring—the heavy gold ring his mother had given him—he reached for her hand and slipped it on her ring finger.

"One day soon I shall come claim it again," he said. "And the hand that wears it."

She remained there beside him for a moment longer. Then, as the huge doors began to open, she clapped her heels to Gracielle and sent her galloping up the dark and narrow street beyond.

There were several things the Princess Alys liked to do herself, after her tiring woman had gone to bed. Plucking her eyebrows was one of them. That is what she was doing now, sitting in front of her looking glass with a tall candle on each side of it. She had paused to admire her handiwork, the thin, proud arch of her brows, and also the clear blue of her eyes under them, when the bedroom door opened and the candle flames swayed and guttered in the draft. She frowned angrily into the glass. "Oh, it's you," she said.

"Yes."

"Where have you been?"

"Away."

"I know that. But where?"

"On a quest."

"Women don't go on quests."

"I did."

"You would. Father was worried sick about you."

"I left a note."

"Yes, but you didn't say much in it. Just that . . ." She looked into the glass again, then swung around. "Saints above, but you're a mess! Look at your face, your hair. What have you been doing to yourself?"

"It's just stain and dye. As a matter of fact, I lost them some time ago, haven't been able to put any on in weeks. A bath will take care of what's left."

"But why . . . ?"

"You said that women don't go on quests. And they don't. But there's no reason why an old crone shouldn't. Who would bother her?" She started for her own room which lay beyond, then paused. "By the way, I have something for you. Here." And she gave Alys a ring, a heavy gold ring.

"Why, thank you," said Alys. She held it to the light, examining it. "It looks familiar."

"Yes."

"You're sure it's for me?"

"Yes," said Lianor. And going into her own room, she shut the door.

CHAPTER TWENTY

FOR THE THIRD time Brian checked the saddle girth, and Gaillard turned and nuzzled him, then tossed his head and stamped his freshly shod hooves.

"Easy," said Brian soothingly. He glanced up at the sun. "It won't be much longer."

Tertius, standing beside him in the innyard, looked up also. Though it had been almost midnight before they had seen to their horses and the pack mule and been shown to their own quarters by the sleepy innkeeper, they had been up at dawn, for they had had much to do. While the stableboy took Gaillard off to the blacksmith's, Brian and Tertius went to the castle armory where the armorer had gone over

Brian's arms, examining his hauberk for worn or doubtful links and replacing the leather ties of his tilting helm. Shortly after that, Sir Amory, the seneschal, had come in. He did not say how he knew Brian was there nor did he ask any questions but, grim and for the most part silent, he had helped him select a new lance—a longer and heavier one than the one Brian had shattered in the town square on Midsummer Day.

Again Brian looked up at the sun, which glowed dully in the winter sky like a worn penny.

"Where is he?" he asked impatiently. "It is past noon."

"Not quite," said Tertius. And, as if to confirm this, at that moment they again heard the harsh, rasping horn blast that had announced the Black Knight's arrival exactly six months before.

They turned, looking out through the arched opening of the innyard. Again there was the sound of horses' hooves, the tramp of many feet, echoing in the narrow street, and the Black Knight and his captain rode past, followed by the ranks of men-at-arms. Seen thus, against the weathered walls of the houses opposite, the Black Knight loomed up like a dark shadow that was larger than a mortal man, the embodiment of night. And though he was only framed there in the archway for a moment, Brian felt the same clutch of dread he had felt when he faced him in the square.

Then he was gone; they were all gone. Tertius turned back to him, searching his face, but Brian avoided his eyes. Acting as squire, Tertius picked up the tilting helm, put it on and laced it into place. He held Gaillard while Brian mounted, handed him his lance and the shield, which the armorer had painted for him early that morning and which no longer bore the Caercorbin arms but was now a bright, blood red. Then he mounted too.

As Gaillard started out of the innyard, Tertius said, "There are many things that I could say to you, but there is only one that is important. Remember that you are not alone."

It was as if Tertius had been reading his mind, and Brian was glad that his face was hidden. For now that the day and the hour had come, it was this that he felt more than anything else: not so much fear of death as a sense that he was alone, more alone than he had ever been in his life. And nothing that Tertius or anyone else said could change that. Nevertheless he nodded and, with Tertius following close behind him, he rode out through the archway and up the street toward the great square.

If anything, the square was more crowded now than it had been on Midsummer Day; the townsmen and those who had been coming in from the countryside all morning standing close-packed about its sides eight or ten deep. As before, the king was on his throne on the church steps with his daughters on either side of him. And as before, directly in front of him was the Black Knight, still and faceless on his huge black stallion, with his captain at his right hand and his men-at-arms behind him. This time, however, all eyes save that of the Black Knight were not on the king and the grim, dark rider, but on the street that led into the square. And when Brian appeared there was a faint sound from the huge throng, a sound that was half murmur and half deep-drawn sigh.

When Gaillard saw the black charger, he tried to quicken his pace and Brian had to hold him hard fighting the bit, as they crossed the open space in the center of the square.

"Who are you and what do you here?" asked the Black Knight's captain.

Brian inclined his head toward Tertius who was now at his side and it was he who answered.

"I am Tertius of Bedegraine and this is Sir Brian of Caercorbin," he said. "As to why we are here, you must surely know that."

"You are challenging the Black Knight?"

This time Brian answered himself by nodding.

"*Sir* Brian," said the captain, accenting the title. "Are you not the squire who fought the Black Knight on Midsummer Day?"

Again Brian nodded.

"And you are now a knight?"

"Yes," said Tertius firmly. "He is now a knight."

"And has changed his blazon, too. Well, it does not matter. Squire or knight, red shield or not, the end will be the same. Take your place."

A moment longer Brian remained there. Now that he was close, he could see how the king had aged in the months since he had last been in Meliot: there were new lines on his face and his hair was more gray than black. He glanced at Alys, who was leaning forward, her eyes shining, then at Lianor. She was sitting still as a statue. And though her face was expressionless, it was pale and her eyes were as dark and troubled as her father's. Brian looked deep into them. Then, raising his lance in salute, he turned Gaillard and sent him cantering across the square to the far end near the street by which he had entered.

The Black Knight, holding his charger on a

tight rein, was walking him to the opposite end of the square with the terrible, controlled slowness that Brian remembered so well. And as Brian waited for him to take his position, the helpless, lost feeling—the feeling that, despite the crowd, he was alone—came over him again. This, he sensed dimly, was one of the reasons that the Black Knight had so far been invincible. For besides his strength and skill, by his own inhuman detachment he was able to isolate his antagonist from everyone and everything else, draw him into the small dark world in which he lived and of which he was the unquestioned master.

A chill came over Brian, a chill that had nothing to do with the bite of the wind. And feeling his strength, his very will, drain from him as sap retreats at the onset of winter, he looked around desperately for something—anything warm and human—that would restore him to the world of the living and to himself. He strained his eyes toward the church steps where he knew he would find what he needed.

And suddenly, much nearer at hand, a face appeared in his narrow field of vision: the unexpected but familiar face of Long Hugh. He was leaning on his bow with Hob and Wat beside him and all their eyes were on him.

Brian blinked, looked again. And now, as if he were looking through Tertius's magic glass, other faces began appearing sharply and clearly out of the blur that was the crowd: the wild, dark face of Migbeg, and standing next to him, Diccon of the Holm with Amy on his shoulders and his wife, Nan, by his side. Again he blinked, peering through the slit of his helmet, and saw the hermit, his brown, wrinkled face sober. And beyond him, towering above Lamorna and everyone else in the crowd, Giles.

"Brian . . ." said Tertius from somewhere behind him.

He looked up. The Black Knight was in position on the far side of the square. And now, suddenly—no longer alone—the chill left him. And just as sensation had returned to his arm when Nimue's serpent had gone from him, so he felt his strength come flooding back, doubled and redoubled. He sat up straighter in the saddle and Gaillard, as if sensing what had happened, neighed shrilly, straining to be off.

The Black Knight's captain, again acting as marshall, raised his sword, glancing from Brian to his master and holding them while a man could count to ten. Then he brought his sword down and, lance couched, Brian drove in his heels and sent Gaillard thundering forward over the cobbles of the square. The lance, longer than any he had ever used before, felt light as a willow wand, and he rode loosely, easily, red shield forward and ready. Then, as the Black Knight loomed up before him, he clamped his legs more tightly, gripped the spear with an iron grip and drove its point at the center of the dark shield. There was a sudden, double shock as both spears struck home and then, as a roar went up from the crowd, he was galloping on with no one before him.

He reined Gaillard in, pulled him about. The Black Knight, lance shattered, lay on his back in the center of the square while his charger, wild-eyed and snorting, circled wide about him, shying away from those who tried to catch his dangling reins.

Slowly, painfully, the Black Knight struggled to his feet. Brian rode back toward him.

"Do you yield?" he asked.

The Black Knight did not answer, but drew his sword and raised his shield, waiting. It was to be to the outrance, then, a fight to the finish. Tertius came cantering up as Brian dismounted.

"Don't, Brian," he said. "You needn't."

"I must," said Brian. "Here." And he held out his lance and Gaillard's reins.

"No," said Tertius. "You have beaten him."

"Not until he yields," said Brian. "Will you take these?"

"No," said Tertius again.

Reversing his spear, Brian drove the point between two cobbles, tied the reins around it.

Then, drawing Starflame, he strode toward the Black Knight.

For a moment they faced one another, the Black Knight poised and still in an awful stillness. And perhaps because of that stillness, or perhaps because they were now closer to one another than they had ever been before, so close that Brian could see every ring in the mail of his hauberk, he was more menacing than he had been when he was mounted. Then the Black Knight struck, a sudden and mighty blow. Brian caught it on his shield, put it aside and struck in his turn. And, as the Black Knight fended it off and struck again, Brian knew that this was no Rufus: this was a strong, skilled and deadly swordsman.

Somewhat taller than Brian, the Black Knight pressed his attack, cutting high and low and sometimes feining, thrusting with his point. Brian gave back before him, warding off and returning each stroke and circling to his left in the hope that he could get past the Black

Knight's guard. But the Black Knight turned with him, his shield always before him, his sword flashing in the sun. They fought thus for some time, the square ringing with the clash of steel. Then gradually, almost imperceptibly, the Black Knight's blows began to come more slowly. And, though he was bleeding from several small wounds, Brian went over to the attack. Striking a great overhand blow, he drove the Black Knight's shield back against him so that he staggered. And, as he recovered, raised his sword, Brian struck again, past the edge of his shield. The blow fell hard and true on the Black Knight's helmet and again he staggered and this time went down. In an instant Brian was on him, Starflame's point at his throat.

"Now do you yield?" he asked.

The Black Knight still did not answer, did not move. Sheathing his sword, Brian drew his dagger, cut the thongs of the Black Knight's helmet and pulled it off.

He was not sure what he expected; possibly

a terrifying face, certainly a dark and evil one. But the face he saw was nothing like that. Though it was gaunt, drawn, and a deep scar cut across the high forehead and disappeared into the graying hair, it was a noble face with a firm chin and aquiline nose. The eyes, closed until now, opened slowly. They were shadowed, clouded, but blue as Brian's own. Seeing Brian bending over him, the knight raised one hand weakly, either in surrender or to push the dagger aside. Brian looked at it, stiffened, then looked again. On one of the fingers was a gold ring: a heavy gold ring wrought in the likeness of a wivern holding his tail in his teeth.

"Where got you that ring?" asked Brian.

Still dazed, the fallen knight looked up at him blankly and did not answer.

Rising, Brian sheathed his dagger, unlaced his own helmet, and tossed it aside. Sensing that the drama that was being played out before them was not yet ended, the huge crowd that filled the square was hushed, waiting. Striding over to the church steps, Brian said, "My Lady Lianor, may I have the ring I gave you last night?"

"Ring?" Her face was inscrutable, her eyes dark, unfathomable. "I have no ring."

"Do you mean this one?" asked Alys, holding out her hand. Brian looked at the ring, at her, and then again at Lianor.

"Yes," he said. "And it please you . . ."

Taking the ring from her, he returned to the Black Knight. He was still lying where Brian had left him, staring up at the wintery sky as if even that was strange, alien. Kneeling beside him, Brian slipped his arm under him and raised him. And as he did, as he held out the ring that was the twin of the one on the Black Knight's finger, there was a sudden shriek from near the church steps.

"Sir Owaine! Oh, my dear . . . !"

Brian looked up as the Lady Leolie burst out of the crowd and ran toward them.

"Mother!" he said. Then to Merlin who

was following her, walking more slowly. "Did you . . . ?"

"Of course," said Merlin. "I thought she should be here—for many reasons—so I brought her."

The Lady Leolie was kneeling now also.

"My dear," she said, her voice choked. "Don't you know me?"

Something was happening to the knight's eyes. They were becoming clearer, brighter.

"Of course I know you, Leolie," he said. "But what do you here? Where is this place?"

"Don't you know?"

He shook his head. "The last thing I remember is a melee near Ascalon. The Saracens had taken us by surprise and we were greatly outnumbered. Sir Guy, Sir Baldwin and Simon were with me . . ."

"I think," said Merlin, "that it is time for some explanations. You," he said to the Black Knight's captain, "tell us what you know."

"Yes, master," said the captain. Then to the

man Leolie now held cradled in her arms, "do you know me, Sir Knight?"

The knight studied him, then said. "No. No. Something teases me as if I should, but . . . no."

"He knew me but an hour ago when I armed him," said the captain somewhat sadly. "I am no surgeon, but I think he has been for many years reft of his wits and is now again as he was before he came to us."

"Came to you where and when?" said Merlin testily. "Tell the whole tale from the beginning."

"Yes, master," said the captain again. "We were in the Holy Land, too, most of my men here and the two brothers, Sir Liam and Sir Dermot. We were on our way home to the North, but when we came here to Meliot, Sir Liam said, 'This is a rich city. We have shed our blood on foreign soil and are going home empty-handed. Why should they not share what they have with us?' So he hove at the ford, demanding toll of the merchants who would cross there."

King Galleron, Lianor, Alys and many others had now joined them.

"This was in the reign of my father?" asked the king.

"Yes, Sire," said the captain. "He was the first Black Knight."

"The first?"

The captain nodded. "He was killed by your father's archers. We searched for his body afterward, found it some distance downstream. Sir Dermot put on his hauberk and helm, becoming the Black Knight in his stead, and rode into Meliot, demanding your father's head."

"Then there were two Black Knights," said Galleron. "I always suspected that. And this man here is . . ."

"No, Sire," said the captain. "For more than ten years Sir Dermot was the Black Knight and collected tribute from you, during which time we rebuilt the keep and made it stronger than ever. Then one day this knight here came riding through the forest. Sir Dermot challenged him, and they fought. It was a fierce battle, but in the end this knight killed him. He was badly wounded, however, so we took him into the keep. And when we tended him, we found that he was . . . strange."

"Strange how?" asked the Lady Leolie.

"He did not seem to know who he was, where he had been or where he was going. It was probably because of this blow," and he pointed to the scar on the knight's forehead. "But since he was an even greater fighter than Sir Liam or Sir Dermot, we said to ourselves, 'Why should he not become the Black Knight?' And so, twice a year, we armed him and, though at other times he was like a man walking in his sleep, once he had his weapons in his hand, he overcame everyone who faced him. Until today."

"Now do you remember?" asked Merlin.

"No," said the knight. "As I told you, the last thing I remember was the melee at Ascalon. The next was a knight, a young knight, who knelt beside me and showed me a ring. . . ."

"My ring," said the Lady Leolie, "the one you gave me and I gave him. And there he stands, your son—our son—Brian."

Though the music, the sound of laughter, was now louder than ever in the great hall, it was quiet in the close; quiet and dark.

"I could not believe it at first," said Brian. "That they were really there. Lamorna had said something about it, of course. But still it must have been Merlin's doing, too."

She was not interested in such things now, but she nodded.

"When did you first know?" she asked.

"Who you were or how I felt about you?"

"Both."

"I think I began feeling this way before we ever left Meliot."

"Liar!"

"It's true."

"You gave no sign of it."

"There was no time. It happened when I looked at you in the solar, the afternoon before we set out. But I didn't realize it until later."

"When?"

"When I found myself thinking about you more and more during our quest."

"And the other?"

"When did I guess who you were? I'm not sure. Perhaps when I asked Tertius if it were possible that you were changing, and he looked at me as if I were a fool. Certainly later, in Nimue's castle. Now you must tell me something. Why did you give your sister the ring?"

"Because I wanted to be sure."

"Of what?"

"Of how you really did feel—about both of us."

"And are you sure now?"

"I think so."

"You only think so?"

"All right, yes. I'm sure."

"Lianor . . ."

"Are they still there?" asked Tertius.

"Yes," said Merlin. "And will be for some time yet."

"It seems odd."

"Why odd?"

"Well, we've been together constantly for quite a long time now, Brian and I. I'm sure you understand."

"That's one of my troubles. I understand everything. It can become very tiresome. Now what were we talking about?"

"You were explaining the difference between a cantrip and a spell."

"There's very little difference."

"There must be some."

Merlin looked at him impatiently. "Nimue wanted it all quickly. 'Never mind the theory, the details. Just tell me how to do it.' But you! All right. I'll tell you, if you'll tell me more about those stars—explain the difference between a quasar and a pulsar."